WAR TALK AT PEACE TALKS

PEACE UNDER DURESS IN SOUTH SUDAN

STEPHEN
PAR KUOL

Africa
World Books
Pty Ltd

ISBN 978-0-6482422-6-0
© Stephen Par Kuol, 2019

Published by Africa World Books Pty. Ltd.

Design and typesetting: All in One Book Design
(www.allinonebookdesign.com.au)

Dedication

This book is dedicated to the eternal memories of my nephew and comrade in arms, Major Tuong Wal Gatluak, who martyred in Bentiu, Unity State on May 5, 2014, my most intimate companion, Sergeant Major Nai Gai Biliew, who perished in that pogrom against Nuer ethnicity on December 17, 2013 in Juba, and ultimately, to the heroic soul of the SPLA (IO) Viva Boys who martyred in J1 bloodbath and at Grampa Park on their miserable journey to the Congo in July 2016.

Debts of Gratitude

Many friends and comrades contributed one way or another in making this piece of work a success. I owe the most to my good friend, Dr. Ann Gloria Evans, who bought me the MacBook Air I used for researching material and redrafting the manuscript after losing the first draft when my previous device failed.

I also owe a debt of gratitude to the secretarial team of the Thematic Join Committee of the SPLM (IO) and the Government delegations under the able hands of Martin Abucha and David Kuaje. Those two young men served me well as the institutional memory of the ARCSS process. The documents they provided refreshed my memory and guided my research and writing.

Furthermore, I cannot thank my comrade and friend, Dr. John Chuol Kuek enough for proofreading the first draft and assessing the cost of publication.

Another good friend, Dr. Gatluak Ter Thach provided valuable academic advice on framing the book format. His brilliant counsel also helped me to efficiently budget for this piece of work during a time of financial hardship.

It also goes without mentioning that I could not complete this work without the wise counsel of my late friend, Honorable Daniel Wuor Joak who uncovered my latent writing skills and encouraged me to document my experiences during the negotiations in a book.

I wish to thank my generous financiers for providing the funds to get the book published. Most specifically, my friends, Ann Gloria and Gregg Brown in the United States.

Above all, I am deeply indebted to my beloved wife, Tabitha and my children, Nyamaar, Kume and Nyantot for putting up with my long absence from the warmth of their love and company in Nairobi while attending peace talks over 20 months plus two years of my diplomatic and media campaign that took me to North America, Europe and Australia to tell our side of story after the July 2016 crisis. I also owe the ultimate debt of gratitude to my elderly parents whom I have left to fend for themselves in their advanced ages at a time when they need my care the most while on the trail to find a lasting peace for South Sudan. I owe the same debt of gratitude to my baby brother, Albino Mawich Kuol whom I left alone to shoulder most of the family responsibilities.

Ultimately, I thank all my friends who provided financial support and put a roof over the heads of my children during my four years of unemployment. They are so many, and sadly, I don't have enough space here to mention all their names.

My many friends and comrades in the United States, Australia, Canada and South Sudan have been truly generous and walked the walk with me until the end. If I failed to accomplish the set goals for this work and the cause that returned us to the bushes of South Sudan and exile in July 2016, it is my own fault and not a lack of support. I thank you all very much!

About the Author

Stephen Par Kuol was a frontline negotiator representing the SPLM (IO) at the Intra-SPLM talks in Arusha, Tanzania right through to the Addis Ababa Peace talks culminating in the ARCSS agreement, the High Revitalization Forum and the Khartoum Track. Prior to that, he served as the Deputy Ambassador of Sudan to the United Republic of Tanzania (2008-2010) and was the Jonglei State Minister of Education (2010-2014).

Stephen Par Kuol is also an academician with an extensive research, writing and teaching background both in the United States and in Africa. He was a visiting lecturer at the Faculty of Law and Social Sciences at Dr. John Garang Memorial University in Bor, Jonglei State. He also served as an Adjunct Professor of Criminal Justice and Social Sciences at the Metro Community College of Omaha for three years (2004-2006).

The author is a diplomat, researcher, poet and freelance writer who has extensively written on the political affairs of South Sudan.

His most recent publications are *South Sudan in the Shadow of Global Transitions, Republic as a Responsibility, Demilitarize the Minds, not the Towns, South Sudan: Another Rwanda in the Making, Towards the Death of the Nascent Nation, Machar Versus the IGAD,* and *The Power We Must Share in Soba.*

Table of Contents

Glossary of Acronyms

ANC	African National Congress
ARCSS	Agreement on The Resolution of The Conflict in The Republic of South Sudan
R-ARCSS	Revitalized Agreement on The Resolution of The Conflict in the Republic of South Sudan.
ACR - AU	Commission of Inquiry Reports
AJMCC	Area Joint Military Ceasefire Committees
AU	African Union
AU COI	African Union Commission of Inquiry
AUHLAHC	African Union High-level Ad hoc Committee
AUSF	Amalgamated Units of the Security Forces of South Sudan
BEFMA	Board of Economic and Financial Management Authority.
BOSS	Bank of South Sudan
BSRF	Board of Special Reconstruction Fund
CoH	Cessation of Hostilities
CoHA	Cessation of Hostilities Agreement
CSO	Civil Society Organizations
CPA	Comprehensive Peace Agreement
CRA	Compensation and Reparation Authority
CRISS	Agreement on the Conflict Resolution in South Sudan
CTRH	Commission for Truth, Reconciliation and Healing
CTSAMM	Ceasefire and Transitional Security Arrangements Monitoring Mechanism
DDR	Disarmament, Demobilization, and Reintegration
DOPS	Declaration of Principles

EFMA	Economic and Financial Management Authority
EDF	Enterprise Development Fund
EITI	Extractive Industries Transparency Initiative
EPRDF	Ethiopian People's Revolutionary Democratic Front
FFAMC	Fiscal and Financial Allocation Monitoring Commission
FDs	Former Detainees also known as G-10
GRSS	Government of the Republic of South Sudan (Pre-Transition Period)
HCSS	Hybrid Court for South Sudan
HLRF	High-Level Revitalization Forum
IBC	Inclusive Boundaries Commission
IDPs	Internally displaced persons
IGAD	Intergovernmental Authority on Development. The Intergovernmental Authority on Development (IGAD) is comprised of seven-member states (Djibouti, Ethiopia, Kenya, Somalia, South Sudan, Sudan, and Uganda). This organization was initially established to engage only on developmental, and environmental concerns.
IGAD PLUS	An expanded form of the IGAD-led Mediation
IMF	International Monetary Fund
IPF - IGAD	Partners Forum
J1	Juba Palace
JIU	Joint Integrated Unit
JMCC	Joint Military Ceasefire Commission
JMCT	Joint Military Ceasefire Teams
JMEC	Joint Monitoring and Evaluation Commission
MVM	Monitoring and Verification Mechanism
NCAC	National Constitutional Amendment Committee
NDC	National Defense Council

NEC	National Elections Commission
NGO	Non - Governmental Organization
NLA	National Legislative Assembly
NPGC	National Petroleum and Gas Corporation
NPTC	National Pre-Transitional Committee
NSC	National Security Council
PCA	Permanent Ceasefire Arrangements
PCTSA	Permanent Ceasefire and Transitional Security Arrangements
POCS	Protection of Civilian Sites
PFMA	Public Financial Management and Accountability Act, 2011
PRMA	Petroleum Revenue Management Act, 2012
PRSF	Petroleum Revenue Savings Fund
R-JMEC	Revitalized Join Monitoring and Evaluation Commission
R-TGONU -	Revitalized Transitional Government of National Unity
R-TNL	Revitalized Transitional National Legislature
SAA	Special Arrangement Area
SDSR	Strategic Defense and Security Review
SPLA	Sudan People's Liberation Army
SPLM	Sudan People's Liberation Movement
SPLM/A	Sudan People's Liberation Movement/Army
SPLM/A (IG)	Sudan People's Liberation Movement/Army (In Government)
SPLM/A (IO)	Sudan People's Liberation Movement/Army (In Opposition)
SPLA MI	Military Intelligence
SPLM/DC	Sudan People's Liberation Movement for Democratic Change
SPLM (FPD)	Former Political Detainees

SRF	Special Reconstruction Fund
SSAO	South Sudan Armed Opposition
SST	Security Sector Transformation
TBC	Technical Boundaries Committee
TCoSS	Transitional Constitution of South Sudan, 2011
TGoNU	Transitional Government of National Unity
TNLA	Transitional National Legislative Assembly
TOR	Terms of References
TROIKA	United States, the United Kingdom and Norway
TTPSU	Transitional Third-Party Security Unit
UN	United Nations
UNHCR	United Nations High Commissioner for Refugees
UNMISS	United Nations Mission in South Sudan
VMT	Verification and Monitoring Team

Introduction

This piece of work emanates from the inside experience of the author who served as a frontline negotiator representing the SPLM/A (IO) from the Addis Ababa Peace Talks in January 2014 right through to the handshake phase between President Salva Kiir and Dr. Riek Machar on July 21, 2018 and the final signing of R-ARCSS in the same capital on September 12, 2018.

Based on his own grasping of the entire peace process, the author attempts to provide in-depth analysis as well as critical reflections on the diplomatic atmosphere under which the talks were conducted in Addis Ababa, Arusha, Entebbe, and Khartoum.

It is a story of intransigence, the tyranny of gun culture and the lack of political will to resolve the national crisis and devastating civil war in South Sudan. The role of the warring parties in the crisis is thoroughly and critically analyzed.

The author also gives insight and perspective on why and how the South Sudanese crisis defeated the parties, the mediators and the international community.

According to the author, the South Sudanese crisis stymied all the players due to the following factors:

The mediation team were deceived into believing that the parties were negotiating to amicably resolve the conflict while what was actually happening in the corridors of those conference halls was always a belligerent war talk, verbal violence and posturing to score points.

One needs to understand the political psychology of South Sudan to grasp the gist of that mutually antagonistic discourse. In other words, one must know South Sudanese elites culturally, politically and intellectually to understand how they fight and what they are fighting over.

As we exposed it in the Arusha Track, the SPLM/A does not have a culture of resolving conflicts by addressing the root causes and principle issues. Managing crises and postponing vendettas to focus on tackling the common enemy (the Jallaba State) had always been the SPLM/A's way of resolving conflicts throughout the liberation period.

Another thing that outwitted the mediation and the so-called friends of IGAD was the cheeky diplomacy of the South Sudanese elites who took advantage of the internal weaknesses of the mediation team and turned peace negotiations into a protracted forum to settle age-old accounts at the expense of the downtrodden people of South Sudan and the foreign friends sponsoring the peace process. The name of the game became vocal participation to avoid sanctions and diplomatic isolation. This combative and intransigent attitude was exacerbated by the negotiators' lack of authority to make substantial concessions.

Nhial Deng, for example, would make eloquent presentations in the Queen's English and masquerade as the Chief Negotiator fully authorized to give and take concessions at the table but in actual fact, he was a mere messenger to pass on belligerent messages from President Kiir to his protagonists (Riek Machar's delegation).

The learned lawyer acted like a defense attorney in a criminal trial court. In strict adherence to the tone and tune of his client, Kiir, Deng was sometimes sarcastic and sometimes diplomatic, it all depends on the mood and whims of his fascist puppeteer.

The historical background of the conflict is significant. Hence, the book covers the mobilization for war, fabrication of the crisis by Kiir as a coup d'état and the IGAD initiative leading to the peace talks that broke down without agreement several times over a period of five years until the presentation of the draft compromise agreement. Even that was to be signed under duress as a 'take it or leave it' ultimatum.

The role of the warring parties is narrated as well as to why and how the South Sudanese Crisis defeated the regional mediation and the international community. The first two chapters tell tales of political violence deeply rooted in the organizational, political and historical culture of the SPLM/A during the time of comrades in the 1980s.

The book walks the reader through the history and magnitude of the crisis and how the leaders of South Sudan and their international partners including IGAD, TRIOKA and the US failed the downtrodden people of South Sudan in all attempts to bring peace.

The author submits that the fundamental root cause of the conflict is the political militarism and culture of war constructed by the environment of the war of liberation spearheaded by the SPLM/A.

Aggravated by a leadership deficit in the person of General Salva Kiir, this culture of war and political violence has reached its apex and it is pushing the nascent nation to the precipice.

In sum, this book is a story of peace talks, which were actually war talks, both at the negotiating tables in various capitals around the region and on the ground in South Sudan.

The chapters are chronologically formatted to give them the correct historical flavor with structural flow. This is critical in order to understand the fundamental root causes of this socially and politically devastating state of affairs. The content of the Agreement on the Resolution of the Conflict in South Sudan is well covered in two chapters: 'The Key Provisions of ARCSS' and 'All Agreements Dishonored'. The rest include analyses and proposals by the author to end the conflict.

CHAPTER ONE

The Synopsis of the Historical Background

 The onus is on us to demonstrate it to ourselves and to the outside world that we are the 'we' that we say we are.

Prof. Walter Kun Ojuok

United by common struggle against common oppression by various forces of imperialism and colonialism, the people of South Sudan have suffered and fought back together from the slave trade resistance in 18th century, through the brutal British pacification wars, to the civil wars with Khartoum based successive regimes until they finally achieved their own independent state on July 9, 2011. Born out of arduous intermittent civil wars, the Republic of South Sudan under the ruling the SPLM/A was confronted by a myriad of transitional challenges in terms of addressing its egregious past as well as forging a new course forward to cohesive and viable nationhood. One of those daunting tasks was the democratization of the political process against the high current of the SPLM/A's culture of political militarism. Preparing the country for independence through establishing state institutions for nation building and referendum was a tall order of challenging and competing priorities. Comrade Pagan Amum Okiech, the SPLM Secretary General and the then Minister for Peace and CPA Affairs in the Government of Southern Sudan, called it an era of multiple transitions.

Prof. Peter Adwok Nyaba, the former Minister of Higher Education put those challenges in his book entitled: *South Sudan: The Crisis of Infancy.*

In his article entitled: *The Root Causes of the December 2013 Crisis,* Comrade Mabior Garang De Mabior stated: "The root cause of the ongoing crisis is the failure of the SPLM/SPLA to redefine the objectives of the movement within the contexts of the new realities of the independent Republic of South Sudan."

The Ugandan academic, Mahmood Mamdani observed: "South Sudan has yet to transition itself to a state since its independence in July 2011."

In a similar vein, I called it a conundrum of the SPLM/A transforming itself into a conventional democratic political party and a conventional professional national army. Although the Transitional Constitution of South Sudan stipulated that the SPLA shall be transformed into the South Sudan Armed Forces and shall be non-partisan, national in character, patriotic, regular, professional, disciplined, productive and subordinated to civilian rule, the liberation army, turned ruling party, remains partisan, ethnic in character, corrupt, and unprofessional to this day.

The political variant dubbed the SPLM Party, has also failed to transition into a conventional democratic political party. It failed to institutionalize itself for governance and nation-building. The liberation movement remained a bush government of kleptocrats ruling the nascent nation through tribal oligarchies and local chains of tribal patronages. Those same rulers and military elites became tyrants ruling with an iron fist and without accountability to the populace. Subsequently, South Sudan attained political independence without the very freedom the people fought for.

Having sacrificed a million souls for freedom over decades, the people of South Sudan's aspirations for a free and democratic state cannot be over-emphasized. Unfortunately, those wishes have been thwarted by the SPLM/A culture of political militarism, which is best, characterized by a rigid structure of power and totalitarianism.

John Garang was brutally honest about it when he stated: "The SPLM/A is a tool to bring about democracy and cannot be the democracy itself. You cannot democratize the tool!" he emphasized.

The paradox lies in the twisted logic that the means to bring about democracy must be undemocratic for it to bring the desired end. One wonders what Dr. Garang would have thought had he lived to see that the means (militarism) that justified the end (democracy) has produced a national disaster of this magnitude in his country.

Under this liberation army turned ruling party, the citizens' participation in the political process is habitually undermined. Coercion instead of persuasion is often the manner by which the SPLM government in Juba engages with the populace in the peripheries. Military language, whose mechanics are all about command, dominates all political discourses in the SPLM/A. This means politics without debate. This has produced nothing but a poli-military party without internal democracy. In this autocratic culture, monologue is preferred to dialogue. Far worse, violence is politics and politics is violence in the SPLM/A.

Modern political science contends that turmoil is inevitable where there is no civility within the body politics of the nation in question. That is precisely what happened in the Republic of South Sudan under the SPLM/A. Through its authoritarianism and tribal-ized militarism, the ruling party caused the world's youngest state to descend into genocidal civil war. A war in which the army split along ethnic lines as the Presidential Guards under the direct command of President Salva Kiir executed pogroms against the ethnic Nuers in December 2013.

Under a jungle state of emergency declared by the President, hailing from Dr. Riek Machar's ethnic group became a death sentence without due process of law in Juba. Even some members of the Dinka community who share racial features and tribal marks with the Nuer were not spared! "Maale" the Nuer word for greeting which mean peace, became the calling card for ethnic cleansing.

The President, who kept reminding the healing nation of the 1991 intra-communal violence episodes, directly commanded his Dootkubeny private tribal militia from the presidential palace to execute pogroms, military vandalism, heinous war crimes and crimes against humanity. All this in the name of fighting a fabricated coup.

That operation of shame dismantled the very core of the historical SPLA and the social fabric of South Sudan. For the worst part, it turned the nation into a society of murderers. Neighbors killed their neighbors. Soldiers representing what was supposed to be the 'national' army lynched their own comrades in arms. Revenge killing against innocent Dinka also happened in some parts of the Upper Nile region where the civilians whose children, families, and relatives were massacred in Juba took the law into their own hands in Akobo, Bentiu, and Malakal.

This is not the first time it happened. In the words of Deng Athuai of the South Sudan Civil Society Network: "The SPLM/A loots the country when it unites and kills the people when it splits." Either way, it has always been disastrous for the common citizen of South Sudan. In any case, the split of December 2013 was even more disastrous than the war with the Northern Sudanese regimes in terms of human lives lost, property destroyed and the rift it created on the social fabric of the people.

Far and wide,the hopes and dreams of the people have been dashed to ashes in this war of self-destruction that has put our country on the precipice of death in its infancy. In fact, our young nation is already in comatose.

The warring parties, SPLM (IG) and SPLM (IO), have engaged in peace talks in Addis Ababa, Ethiopia since January 2014. All the attempts to resolve the crisis have yielded nothing positive, as all the agreements signed have been dishonored.

One critical and fundamental question is: Why can South Sudanese political leaders not resolve this senseless conflict? The answer is precise and simple. The SPLM/A has never engaged in a genuine dialogue with itself since it was incepted. Even the engagement under the auspices of IGAD was merely more posturing for war. Everything, including the political system, is a product of war.

According to Dr. Nyaba: "South Sudan is ruled by war-made politicians." By that he means that we are a product of war politics. Being an alien concept, peace comes when it comes. We don't make it. South Sudanese seldom give themselves an opportunity to agree or disagree as they operate with closed minds.

In this autocratic culture, dialogue is loathed and dreaded. It is a culture of silence that kills silently. Even constructive criticism is misconstrued as an insult. A critical pen like that of Isaiah Abraham is feared more than a bazooka. It is an immensely tragic reality and we are exceptionally good at it.

It has been observed that the first casualty of war is often the truth. Speaking from my ARCSS and HRF experiences, I would further argue that another casualty of war is the trust. Trust among South Sudanese communities has been eroded by the raging tribal war of words and weapons. That has severely ravaged social fabric of society making trust-building a daunting task.

"There is truth only in the wine." say the French. In our war weary nation, our truth is in war. We truly fight but make false peace. Evidently, the South Sudanese have become accustomed to the illusion of security that your insecurity is my security and your death is my life. We talk war and sign war in the disguise of peace as we did with ARCSS and so many other agreements dishonored during the conflicts.

The gestures of our violent culture speak volumes more to our state of mind than to our actions. One such action was the specter of Salve Kiir's daughter's wedding where he and Dr. Machar jointly gave hand of their daughter to the groom with prayers and broad smiles while an ambush was being laid to assassinate Machar that same evening at the order of Kiir.

Another disgusting act was that a joint press conference was held by both men during the J1 bloodbath while their soldiers were butchering each another just outside the fences of the Presidential Palace.

The two leaders called for calm while the President knew damn well that it was violence initiated by none other than himself. He later shamelessly claimed that Machar took in a pistol to murder him. Anyone who knows Riek Machar would never believe such a cheap charge. In this nasty game of political violence lies are white but the truth is murky. Political violence is a game of shameless white lies in South Sudan. We call it "Politikac" in Thok Nath (political lie).

My own candid observation as a student of the social sciences is that the South Sudanese have huge social capital without, the critically needed political capital to make peace. That puzzled many foreign diplomats who watched us interacting in those corridors of Addis Abababa conference halls where we laughed and joked like sane and civilized at teatime but fought like mad cats at the peace table. That is exactly what I mean by the book title. Deng Alor Kuol and I call it "Mal me tot" ('little peace' in Thok Nath).

My good friend, Comrade Mabior Garang used to say "Yien ca mouth pion cin yiec til." In Thuok Monyjieng (the Dinka language) this roughly means: "Greeting with a pure heart. One without jealousy or grudges." The Dinka and Nuer have a common saying that animosity is never in the teeth but deep in the chest of men.

That means you can smile it out with someone but still hate him or her under your breath.

With the South Sudanese, it is the George Bush version of diplomacy. You are either bad or good. Nothing exists in between. This results in extreme intolerance of differences and makes it difficult to reach a negotiated political settlement. Our approach to conflict resolution is zero-sum. It is a winner takes it all game and there is no soul-searching mechanism for self-criticism. We see things through an "I am right, and you are wrong" lens.

This mentality entails why we have been locked in a protracted war of self-destruction that has eroded the common national identity we have been laboring so hard to forge. Even the sovereignty we were clamoring for is diminishing in our watch. That is why in shame and anguish, we have been flocking to seek refuge in the same country (Sudan) whose citizenship we renounced to create our own state in January 2011.

At home in South Sudan, we have been reduced to destitutes and displaced within the promised land of milk and honey. The question lingering in so many heads is: "What is it that we must do to reverse this tragic cycle of abyss and doom?"

The answer is simple and clear. We must demilitarize our minds and adopt the culture of dialogue. We must reach an amicable resolution to this conflict based on a win-win solution for a long-lasting peace in South Sudan. Ultimately, we must invoke the wisdom of Dr. Walter Kun Ojuok, that we must practically demonstrate that we are the South Sudanese nation we have been telling the world we are and that we are deserving of statehood. Failure to do so will result in losing the very sovereignty Kiir's regime has been using as a shield to protect itself.

CHAPTER TWO

Etymological Root Causes

> " *A hungry hyena will only run away only if it is called by its name 'hyena' or, it will kill. That is what happened in South Sudan. The culprit (SPLM) has dug the South Sudanese into a long dark tunnel and it has not been called out by its name.*
>
> Akol Liai Mager

For every war, there are always root causes as well as immediate causes. In attempts to resolve conflicts, brokers are often deceived by the immediate causes and try to address them piecemeal. This means ignoring the long period of time spent in mobilization and gestation before that war erupted. That is the delicate fine line between war and conflict.

In most cases, war is an explosive expression of a long-internalized conflict. In other words, you can have conflict without war, but the mere absence of war does not mean the virtual prevalence of peace. Those of us who were born into conflict and lived the practical experience of South Sudanese liberation wars know that it is easier to start a war than to end it. Once it engulfs the country, it can be a protracted madness whereby people wade through life in a constant state of fear.

Hence, peacemaking must be first and foremost conceptualized as a long process and not an event that brings immediate results. It demands genuine soul searching and trust-building over time. All th veterans of the SPLM/A know quite well that the ongoing crisis has its deep roots in the bloody legacy of war of liberation that was punctuated by splits, fratricidal killing, heinous atrocities against the civil population, and perpetual inter-factional infighting spanning over two decades.

As such, the crisis of December 2013 was a culmination of prior grievances that had not been fundamentally resolved. Here is a bit of background:

In its humble origin, the SPLM/A was incepted by military officers from the Sudanese Army under the able leadership of Colonel John Garang De Mabior. Colonel John Garang was one of the integrated officers of Anyanya I. In fact, the SPLM/A was offspring of the Anyanya I and Anyanya II that mutinied in Akobo in 1975 and established their headquarters in Bilpham.

With the help of Ethiopian socialist oriented junta that was running the country with iron fist, Garang and his colleagues, namely William Nyuon, Kerbino Kuanyin, Salva Kiir and others dislodged the Anyanya II forces from Bilphm and replaced them with the SPLM/A in 1983. The civilian politicians could only watch the game. They eventually joined the new movement after Samuel Gai Tut, Akuot Atem and William Abdala who were pushed out of Ethiopia. It was fully incepted later in 1983 as a political-military organization under the patronage of Colonel Mangistu Hailemariam, the President of the Provisional Military Government of Ethiopia.

Being more of a liberation army than a political movement, its most powerful organ was the Political-Military High Command. Thus, the supremacy of the SPLA over the SPLM was not only pronounced, but also fully practiced.

Veteran civilian politicians like Martin Majar, Joseph Odhuoh, Benjamin Bol Akok, and others who insisted on a separation between the armed wing (SPLA) and the political wing (SPLM), or subordination of the SPLA to the SPLM, were arbitrarily detained and brutally tortured. Many of them perished in the SPLA's bush jails.

To militarize all the minds and mold every cadre into military discipline, military training in Bonga was made mandatory to all. Subsequently, the organizational culture of the SPLM/A became that of political militarism.

Under the leadership of Dr. John Garang as the Chairman of the SPLM and Commander In Chief of the SPLA, there were two variants of the movement: the military variant and the political variant. The political variant (SPLM) was deliberately subordinated to the military variant (SPLA) within the structure of the vanguard movement. The SPLM/A has always been militaristic and authoritarian in its organizational discipline and culture. As in any conventional military culture, dissension is rebellion and it is brutally dealt with.

The SPLM/A behaved like a herdsman demanding nothing but obedience from his flock. This culture of guns and militarism has always been glorified just like the violence itself.

The SPLA gunman was both admired and hated in the countryside. In another word, he was seen as a liberation hero, a terrible oppressor, and a looting machine at the same time.

Early on, the SPLA developed an overt disdain for the common unarmed civilian. The SPLA committed heinous atrocities and oppressed the population wherever it set feet and boots in South Sudan.

Even the noble word in Arabic language mousin (citizen) was turned into derogatory term. The supposedly liberation army developed that tendency to scorn the very people it claimed to be liberating.

The SPLM/A was born in Nuer lands in 1983 and the host community of Gajaak Nuer was among the first victims of its wrath. It committed similar atrocities against the Toposa, Murel, Mundari and the Dinka Bor communities. Literally, the SPLA means "people's army" but it rarely conducted itself like one. If any thing, it behaved more like an occupation force within its controlled enclaves.

William Adam observed that: "The reason why you separate the army from the police is because one fights the enemy of the state, the other serves and protects the people. When the military becomes both, the enemy of the state tends to become the people."

That was exactly how the SPLA behaved among the communities during the war and that made it easier for Khartoum to advance its counter-insurgency recruitment missions in Southern Sudan during that period.

Being a peasant army from underdeveloped rural Southern Sudan, mass illiteracy among the forces was another detrimental factor. As we witnessed in so many ways, illiteracy and militarism can be a virulent combination. This combination breeds nothing but corrupt tribal warlords.

For liberating the country and bringing about independence, the SPLA rewarded itself with the largest portion of the national budget. Forty percent of the national budget was spent on the rogue security sector that tends to cause more insecurity in the country. Too little was therefore earmarked for the provision of social services and infrastructure. This type of spending by the SPLM/A Governement has resulted in the failure to deliver social services and the development that the majority of South Sudanese desperately need. In sharp contrast with John Garang's vision of taking "towns to the people" the SPLM(IO) political leadership in the government has completely neglected the peripheries. Ninety percent of the national budget has always been spent in Juba. The rest of the country's share is a mere drop in the ocean. The impoverished states of South Sudan without local revenue bases have been condemned to poverty and underdevelopment by the SPLM/A central government in Juba.

The result has been widespread discontent and dysfunctional political representation manifesting itself in the violence the SPLM is historically known for.

As one writer and researcher put it correctly. "South Sudan is an army with a nation, not a nation with an army". True,we had over 800 generals in the SPLA even before the recent mass promotion by both Pagak and Juba. As in Nazi Germany, the most prestigious (and common) title in South Sudan is "General." Perhaps, one needs those stars on his shoulder to be politically complete and secure.

Call it politicization of the military or the militarization of politics if you will. In this political culture, a political leader without an armed tribal militia behind him is a laughing stock at the mercy of the commander in chiefs.

As mentioned afore, the autocratic culture of the SPLM/A is the etiological root cause of the ongoing conflict. It is so deeply rooted in a culture that loathes dialogue. This makes the movement prone to splits and perpetual infighting.

Historically, the movement spilt several times during the course of the liberation and was reunified without real dialogue to resolve the fundamental causes of the splits that consumed its founding leadership. This culture of silence has been both costly and fatal in term of human lives.

The founding leaders of the SPLA including Samuel Gai Tut, Kerbino Kuanyin Bol, William Nyuon Bany, William Abdala Chuol Deng, Joseph Odouh, Paul Anadi Othow, Akuot Atem all died in the SPLM/A fratricidal killing fields over two decades.

The rest, including veteran politicians like Martin Majar (or Majier) Gai, Benjamin Bol Akok, Joseph Malath, Victor Bol Ayuol-Nhom, Martin Makur Alew, Lokurnyang Lado and many others died in the SPLA bush jails in the brutal hands of none other than General Salva Kiir himself (who was then the SPLA Intelligence Chief).

Statistically, SPLM/A killed its own more than it killed its erstwhile enemy during the long liberation war. One writer termed it as self-gnawing. During the twenty-two years of the liberation struggle, the SPLM/A spent 16 years primarily fighting itself. Very reminiscent of the afterbirth of Communism in Russia during the last century.

Hence, the historical SPLM/A has always been managing crisis after crisis. The only thing the SPLM/A factions did each time they reunified their ranks was postponing violent confrontation to focus on confronting the common enemy (Khartoum).

The internal conflict was then left simmering to observe what the SPLM/A leaders called the 'unity of purpose' to fight the common enemy. It was reunified under John Garang again in 1988. It then split again in 1991 after the Nasir Declaration and was reunified in 2002 under Garang after years of bitter inter-factional warfare.

The differences within the SPLM resurfaced at the 2nd National Convention in May of 2008. Salva Kiir, the then Chairman of the SPLM and President of the Government of Southern Sudan, unilaterally decided that he did not want Dr. Riek Machar, to remain as the First Deputy in the SPLM. Instead, he wanted the 2nd Deputy, James Wani Igga, installed in that role.

He failed to give a convincing explanation as to why. He simply did not like him. During the 2002 merger of the SPLM (led by Dr. Garang) and the SPDF (led by Dr. Machar), it was decided as a matter of unity for the people of South Sudan, that the original SPLM line of hierarchy should be used by the re-unified SPLM.

The other position was that there were two movements, SPLM and SPDF, merging. As such, if the leader of one group took the first position, the leader of the other would take the second position, and so on.

Eventually, it was agreed that there were not two movements. There were only two factions of the SPLM. As such, the first position was adopted. Garang was Chairman, Kiir was the 1st Deputy Chairman (since Kerbino and William Nyuon had died), Machar was the 2nd Deputy Chairman (since those who had been between him and Kiir had also died), and Igga was the next in the line of succession (since Lam Akol was out of the SPLM at the time of the reunification).

It was this same formula that the movement used after the passing of John Garang, on July 30, 2005. The SPLM, as a group, had no real intention ever again of bringing this formula to use. During the convention, it became apparent that Kiir and his supporters (such as Paul Malong Awan, Daniel Awet Akot and others) wanted to discard it for reasons better known to themselves.

Ultimately, he failed, and the hierarchy of the SPLM was preserved one more time.

In 2010, national elections were conducted. Salva Kiir appointed Igga as head of a committee whose job was to identify and organize for nomination, the candidates who would be on the SPLM ticket.

As a result, the Party on the basis of their loyalty to Kiir, chose unpopular candidates against the will of the masses. It resulted in several individuals favored by the people declaring as independents. Kiir and his group took that as a threat. Never a good thing if you wanted to stay alive.

The SPLM/A leadership authorized open hostility against them. Machar and a few others were the only ones who felt that the independents had a constitutional right to run for office within their respective constituencies. That did not go down well with Kiir and his handpicked members of the Political Bureau.

Machar was accused of working against the Party and then treated with disrespect by not being allowed to take any active role in the nomination process. In fact, his nomination as Kiir's presidential running mate came as a surprise to Kiir's closest allies who had the understanding that the election was the right time to leave him out in the cold.

However, there were very strong voices on the street warning the President not to make the mistake of leaving him out. Kiir had to listen to those voices. The referendum process leading to independence needed Dr. Machar in the leadership circle of South Sudan for the purposes of legitimacy.

In the end, the elections were rigged against the independent candidates and resulted in rebellions throughout the country. Well known among these included ones led by George Athor Deng, Gatluak Gai, and David YauYau. The December 2013 crisis was just a continuation of that long cycle of violence.

South Sudan under the SPLM/A is a pathological, violent and traumatized nation. It is armed to teeth against itself and is set on a course of self-destruction by the very generation that founded it as an independent state. The legacy of perpetual war has constructed a socio-political culture of violence which is deeply engraved in the psyche of this generation.

The crops of political and military leaders who are still at the helm come from that bush school which esteems only violent militarism.

Worse yet, this culture of guns and political violence has produced a militarized and politicized tribalism within the rank and file. South Sudanese within the SPLM/A have been presenting a bogus sense of nationhood. The paradox of all paradoxes is that South Sudanese in the SPLM/A were fighting for a national cause under tribal nationalism and localism that tended to prevail over the shallow show of patriotic nationalism.

The formation of SPLA battalions and divisions followed geographic and ethnic lines. This happened in part because 'recruits' (both volunteers and those who were forced) coming in waves from regions directly impacted by the fighting. As the war progressed, these military groupings continued to reflect their regional origins, with commanders specifically chosen to lead people from their home areas.

That bred nothing but local warlords and further fragmentation of the united nationalism that necessitated the liberation struggle in the first place. During the armed struggle for independence, the glue that kept the various forces of the SPLM intact was their common enemy and their aspirations for self-determination and independence.

Post-independence, that glue was not strong enough to hold them all together. Being the de facto political and administrative power in Southern Sudan over two decades the SPLM/A had created South Sudan in its own image.

There has always been a nation and that nation is the SPLM/A. This delusional concept is permanently engraved in the minds and hearts of this political and military generation that the SPLM/A is South Sudan and South Sudan is the SPLM/A. That was why the SPLM/A flag was made the national flag.

Sociologically, the cultural environment created by the protracted armed struggle has immersed generations of our children in violence. Subsequently, they are socialized, oriented and politically educated to be more militant than civil. Civility is thusly not in the vocabulary of our political discourse. This culture has produced that autocratic, ethnocentric, oppressive and corrupt state known as the Republic of South Sudan today. It was stillborn as a failed state under the politically and morally bankrupt leadership of Salva Kiir Mayardit and the web of cronies who groomed him into tyranny, corruption and kleptocracy.

I have written extensively on this predicament.

Two articles stand out: *Republic as a Responsibility* and *The Tribal War of Words on the Worldwide Web*. The point I tried to drive home in those and others is that South Sudan is dangerously militarized and ethnically politicized.

I forecast in 2008 the genocide that happened in December 2013. Those who have read my articles might have seen me as a prophet of doom.

As experiences elsewhere have shown, genocide is inevitable where negative ethnicity is used to mobilize political support. It is even more prevalent where every political conflict is militarized, and every military confrontation is politicized and tribalized. Being a society of violent militants, we tend to posture for war at exactly those times a situation should be addressed peacefully. That is why I maintain that the South Sudanese crisis cannot be resolved without addressing this militaristic mentality. It is the etiological root cause of the ongoing conflict.

~

The author defines the root causes of post-independence conflict as the SPLM/A culture of political militarism that caused several splits during the liberation struggle for independence.

The painful legacies of those inter-factional conflicts and the wounds they inflicted on the social fabric of South Sudanese society have not been healed.

CHAPTER THREE

The Panorama of the Events that Accelerated the Crisis

 Power tends to corrupt, and absolute power tends to corrupt absolutely.

Lord Acton

The Era of Rule by Decrees

The thirteen years of President Salva Kiir's tyrannical reign will go down in the history of South Sudan as an era of 'Rules by Decrees and Leadership Crises.'

In his poetic writing, the journalist, Jon Pen de Ngong has called it "Kiirisis."(Kiir's crisis,). Having failed to provide the leadership to unite his own ruling party through persuasive means, Kiir resorted to rule by decrees without adhering to the party rules and the national constitution.

Through those tormenting presidential decrees, the crisis was seen looming high on the horizon very early in 2013.

We all saw it coming! What we did not know was when and how it would descend upon the war weary nascent nation.

As I vividly remember, it was all spectacularly presented via the omnipotent oratory of Ms. Rejoice Sampson, the SSTV household anchor whose appearance with presidential decrees used to send shock waves down the spine of the nation. Utilizing his pen before utilizing his guns, President Kiir unleashed the terror that trembled the guts of his political opponents in the country.

Fear lurked on every nook. For the politicians in the SPLM Government, it was political roulette. You never knew who could be next in the list for appointment or disappointment. "I General Salva Kiir Mayardit decree the relieving of so and so and decree the appointment of so and so" became the only reason to watch Kiir's SSTV at that time.

As the journalist Jacob Akol observed: "The nation was apparently made to believe that Salva Kiir was the law of the land." True, he became so in the manner of Louis the 14th of France. A closer parallel might be to those guillotined in the aftermath of the French Revolution. Kiir was the state and the state was Kiir.

By April 2013, President Kiir embarked on undoing the elections of 2010 by unconstitutionally dismissing elected governors and members of parliament without any reference to the institutions concerned. Ones such as the party, the elected parliaments of the states and the national parliament.

Everyone he did not trust to support him, from Dr. Riek Machar down the line to all the elected governors, were dismissed. Kiir used Article 101 of the Transitional Constitution to legitimize himself and delegitimize his political rivals. All this he did with a straight face. Then he declared war on democracy and anyone else who would dare to stand in the way of his ambition to recreate South Sudan in his own image.

In no time, we found ourselves subjected to a veritable arsenal of military firepower, government surveillance and a full-blown police state. The rest is history of pogroms and mass killings that led to the civil war. In the process, Kiir has made the SPLM, the constitution, and state institutions established by the constitution, irrelevant.

He thus deliberately abandoned all the constitutionally

mandated public institutions including the national army (SPLA) and invested heavily only on his private tribal killing machines such as the previously mentioned Dotkubany, the Mathiang Anyor, and the National Security Agency, he single-handedly established from his bush heyday to eliminate leaders in the SPLM/A.

Kiir has also politicized the civil service and institutionalized mediocrity, nepotism, and corruption in national public institutions.

Straight-faced, he institutionalized tribalism by syndicating his Jieng Council of Elders (JCE) to serve as a law-giving institution and a shadow cabinet.

The rest of the 63 ethnicities were virtually condemned to a second-class citizenship at the whim of the ruling Jieng in our ethnocentric police state. Only those who have accepted eternal servitude and their lower caste status as subjects of the ruling tribe are accommodated in this tribal establishment.

Dissenters, be they Jieng or not, face the violent wrath of Kiir's hoodlums. It goes without informing the records that Kiir ordered his first atrocities against the Jieng community of Luach in Khorfulus County during his war with George Athor in 2011. The first journalist to be murdered by his hoodlums was a young Jeing man by the name of Isaiah Abraham from Twic East County in Jonglei State. Kiir does not subscribe even to ethnic solidarity whenever he deems that he been crossed, or his power is threatened.

The Thanksgiving and Self-Assessment Mission

As mentioned in the previous pages, Salva Kiir's tyrannical actions resurrected the ghosts of unresolved SPLM internal squabbles left simmering since 1983,but the crisis was accelerated by the Thanksgiving Mission of March 2013. This brought the SPLM/A face to face with the populace for the first time in twelve years.

The goal of that nationwide mission was twofold. One was to thank the people of South Sudan for supporting the liberation struggle spearheaded by the SPLM/A. The other was to ask the people to give their performance assessments on governance and delivery of services under them as a ruling party since 2005.

The SPLM issued a report after the survey was conducted and the results were shocking. There was an additional one undertaken by a USAID sponsored agency named Deliot. It reported even worse findings. In both reports, the people of South Sudan expressed loudly and clearly that the SPLM had miserably failed to govern due to a loss of vision and direction under the leadership of President Salva Kiir.

Following this report, the high-ranking members of the SPLM, especially members of the Political Bureau, started thinking of ways to improve the image of the party. One of those was for Kiir to step aside and allow someone else to take over the party's chairmanship. It was felt to be a move that would rejuvenate the party.

The high-ranking party members who expressed interest in running for the office of the chairman included Dr. Riek Machar, Pagan Amum and Rebecca Nyandeng. James Wani Igga indicated his interest for the position, but only if Kiir chose to step aside. Otherwise, he would run for the second position behind Kiir.

The remaining three would challenge Kiir in the 3rd National Convention to take place in May of 2013.

The option of Kiir stepping aside appeared to have traction with a majority of members of the Political Bureau. The popularity of this option prompted Kiir to delay the convention. He needed enough time to manipulate members of the Political Bureau and did so by appointing his supporters to ministerial positions and firing others who appeared less supportive.

Each time that a Political Bureau meeting was scheduled to discuss party documents that were due for endorsement, it was postponed. Each time a meeting was postponed, he used the time in between to work on getting a majority. That way he could go to any meeting comfortable that his version of party documents would get the endorsement that he needed.

Of course, his versions were written in such a way that they gave him an unfair advantage over his would-be rivals. He did such things as setting aside a percentage of the electorate for the chairman. This was joined by other unfair and manipulative acts.

However, unlike past machinations, the strategy of buying people off with ministerial positions was not working anymore. Each time a person was decreed out of their position, they migrated straight to the opposition. He created an artificial clique within the Political Bureau that would blindly back Salva Kiir and only Salva Kiir.

Having realized the shortcomings of getting his way through presidential decrees, he was forced to devise a new strategy. His last resort was to target some members of the Political Bureau for criminal prosecution. Kiir saw this as the only way to take them out of the voting process entirely. The easy prey in this vicious witch-hunt became Pagan Amum, Deng Alor and Kosti Manibe.

The plan was to bog them down with malicious trumped-up criminal charges without taking them to trial for as long as possible. Thusly, they could not participate in Political Bureau proceedings or the Convention. The ultimate intent was to reduce the size of the opposition to an ineffectual body.

Some disgruntled members of the Political Bureau, Riek Machar, Rebecca Nyandeng, Taban Deng, John Luk (and others) could not be neutered using these quasi-legal maneuvers. Conversely, as a way to perceived safety, others such as Nhial Deng, Deng Athorbei and Paul Mayom Akech, abandoned Machar's group after intense consultations with the Jieng Council of Elders.

Several desperate schemes were also deviced to push those remaining out as being irrelevant to the process. However, things were not to be that easy. Having lost influence in the party leadership, Kiir was left only with his executive powers in the government to take decisive action against his political opponents. His next move was to embark on further weakening their positions through further presidential decrees.

Kiir's first action was to withdraw the executive powers he delegated to his Deputy in the government, Dr. Riek Machar on April 15, 2013.

The order did not state any reason for the action. It did not also explain to the public the difference between such powers and the ones stipulated in the Article 105 of South Sudan Transitional Constitution, 2011. This is the Article which gives the vice-president ceremonial powers to act for the president in order to perform any functions or duties conferred upon the president in the event that he or she is out of the country

You don't need a legal background to understand that the decree was an unconstitutional action being used to fight his rival. Politically speaking, it was clearly understood as a punitive action against Machar's intention, made clear during the last Political Bureau meeting, to run for the SPLM chairmanship in the upcoming convention.

Using his executive powers in the government, the President then went on to issue another decree dissolving the national reconciliation committee and canceling the entire process, which was being overseen by Machar.

The convention was initially planned to start on April 18 but was pushed back to June on the grounds that more preparation time was needed.

In late November, Kiir dissolved the structure of the SPLM itself with the exception of his office. He also dissolved the secretariat, as it was already minus its Secretary General, Pagan Amum, whom he had already put under home arrest and a travel ban. The Political Bureau, National Liberation Council, and other state structures were also dissolved. This action was grossly unconstitutional. The SPLM Constitution stipulated that SPLM structures can be dissolved only by a convention. It is the highest organ in the party and the same vehicle that elected him and other leaders in the convention of 2008.

To manipulate the delegates to the convention, Salva Kiir instructed the state governors, after the Governors Forum, to go back to their respective states and start organizing their people. He told them to choose delegates to attend the 3rd National Convention that he and his supporters in the Political Bureau on one side and the National Secretariat on the other were in the process of organizing.

Kiir then decided to sideline the Political Bureau altogether and started working with his loyalists to organize the convention. Having felt that he had maintained the grip of the process through his cronies in the party secretariat, he ordered that National Liberation Council meeting be convened to approve documents of his choosing. Once that was done, he could go ahead with a National Convention in which he would be automatically elected Chairman. An election that would ensure his placement as the Party's flag-bearer come the 2015 presidential vote.

There was more than a bit of a paradox due to the pesky fact that the National Liberation Council was called to meet 'after' it had been dissolved. The mind-boggling question being pondered by all was: "Where did it get legitimacy after the dissolution?"

Salva Kiir had not even attempted to reconstitute it before the meeting could take place. Was he the only legitimizing/delegitimizing factor in the SPLM? Did it simply depend on what he wanted to achieve? The precise and concise answer was that Kiir was now a full-blown dictator both in the party and the government.

That was when Dr. Machar and his group felt that the President had gone too far towards destroying the democratic political process. They called for a press conference to take place on December 6, 2013. There, the general membership of the party and the people would be informed of the status regarding outstanding political issues in the party.

The press was briefed as planned. The point was to convince Kiir that what he had done regarding the structure of the SPLM was unconstitutional and that he had to recognize the legitimacy of the National Liberation Council's right to deliberate on the documents. It was also stated that he must call a Political Bureau meeting before the meeting of the National Liberation Council so that the former could set the agenda for the latter.

Machar's faction ended the briefing by announcing that they would engage the public directly on December 14th if Kiir and his group failed to do the right thing.

Kiir's cronies, under the leadership of James Wani, the Vice President, held their own press conference in response.

Its content was violent and provocative. The statements directly accused Dr. Machar and his people of plotting a coup and very sternly warned them to refrain from playing with fire.

Nevertheless, the constitutional challenges put forward by the forces of democratic change under the leadership of Machar became difficult for Kiir and his followers to ignore. This tends to happen when you have dissolved the structures of the party and are now calling on one of the dissolved structures to legitimize documents intended to shun the democratic process.

The highest executive structure of the party, the Political Bureau, was bypassed in the process that was unfolding. However, even though sidelined, it had the constitutional authority to give legitimacy to the actions of the seemingly favored structure when it came to the agenda for the latter's deliberations.

To solve this mess of contradictions, a mock Political Bureau meeting was quickly called for the pro-Kiir members of the body and blessed Kiir's program in relation to the National Liberation Council meeting.

The initial date set for the meeting of the National Liberation Council was missed due to Kiir's attendance at the memorial service for Nelson Mandela. It was rescheduled.

In a confrontational spirit, the pro-Kiir faction chose to have their meeting to take place on the same day that Dr.Machar's group had chosen for their public rally. That was a clear signal that something malevolent was going to take place on that day and that they could use it to involve the police. They might have been planning for a violent confrontation between their supporters and those of the pro-democracy group. This way, Kiir had an opportunity to put his political rivals in prison on the pretext that they were behind the violence.

Alarmed by the unfolding situation, church and community leaders took the initiative to talk to the leaders on both sides, asking them not to allow their planned activities to coincide. Seeing the genuineness of that appeal, and perhaps in line with their desire to present a clean democratic challenge to the dictatorship without allowing Kiir to make any criminal accusations against them, members of the pro-democracy group resolved to cancel their rally even though that event had been planned prior to Kiir's.

The pro-Kiir sect went ahead with the National Liberation Council meeting. It was even attended by some members of the democracy group, including Dr. Machar.

At that meeting, it became crystal clear that Kiir was not ready for an inclusive and democratic process.

In his opening speech, Kiir made two statements that stood out from all others regarding the opposition. The first gave an indication that Kiir was not ready to tolerate any political challenge. "In recent developments, some comrades came out to challenge my executive powers. I am not prepared to allow this to happen again."

In analyzing this short statement, three connotations are crucial. They are "recent developments", "executive powers" and "not prepared to allow".

The problem is that party activities and presidential powers do not blend but Kiir well often confuses the two to achieve his get his dictatorial way in the party and vice versa.

Kiir also stated that he was "not prepared to allow" a challenge to his powers, "whether in the party or in the government." This speaks for itself. Now we knew that he was fully prepared and ready to fight his political enemies at all costs and using all means available at his disposal to maintain power, however irrelevant and illegal.

The significance was that he was totally willing to use the armed forces as the commander-in-chief to silence his enemies in the party or elsewhere.

A further statement was directed, as an attack on Machar's position and status within the SPLM. It went as follows: "After being accommodated in the SPLM, they took their positions in the government for granted. When they were reshuffled, they took the changes negatively."

By being accommodated, he meant the reunification between Dr. Machar's group and Dr. Garang's faction in 2002. He wanted to send a message that Riek was not a true member of SPLM and as such should not be able to challenge him. Kiir was essentially stating that considered himself as the only true SPLM member deserving of the position.

In truth, Dr. Machar was not being accommodated when he took up the third position after Garang and Kiir. He was only occupying his rightful place in the hierarchy of the movement. Salva himself was among the proponents of that arrangement, for he saw that there was a good chance that he would have been overtaken by Riek if another method was used.

By saying that positions were taken for granted, he wanted the audience to think that Dr. Machar opposed him because he had been shuffled out. He said this while fully realizing that the members knew very well that Machar had made his ambition for the top position known in the party before the reshuffle. In fact, Riek was fully aware that Salva Kiir was going to dismiss him as the only way to discipline. The most interesting question was: "How could he now be accused of rebelling for being reshuffled out when his opposition statements preceded the reshuffle?" It is just mind-boggling.

Having seen Kiir acting tyrannically on the first day of the meeting, the members of the opposition group opted to stay away from the following one the next day.

Dr. Machar told me the news after prayers at Jebel Presbyterian Church that day while leaving for home. It seemed he did not see the danger of boycotting the Sunday session. As would be known later, Kiir certainly saw it as a challenge to his authority. By then, he was left only with his presidential power in the government to arrest his rivals in the party.

Since taking power, Kiir has always contended with plots, real, perceived, imaginary and fake to remove him politically or by force. Over time, he came to rely on a small group of loyalists. In doing so, he alienated the SPLA proper that formed the core of what is supposed to be the national army.

Upon realizing this, Kiir focused on building a loyal National Security Service and presidential guards that he could count on to protect his power. That is where the urgency of Dotkubeny protecting and shoring up the president emanated from. When the General Chief of Staff, James Hoth Mai refused to involve the army in what he saw as a political issue that only needed a political solution, Kiir created his own army.

To proceed with his plan of action, Kiir bypassed Hoth, who had just returned from a long vacation in Australia and instructed his trusted officer in charge of the Presidential Guard, Maj. General Marial Chinoung, to carry out the arrest of his political rival Machar.

Before proceeding with his mission, General Marial had a problem to tackle. The presidential guard was a mixed force, which included members of the Nuer. Since the operation was mainly against Machar, the Nuer soldiers were not trusted for the job.

Not only were they not to be trusted but were also thought to be a serious obstacle to success. Thusly, they had to be disarmed before the operation could be executed.

It was decided that only the Dinka members of the force should carry out the operation, as they were believed to be loyal to their tribesman, Kiir. The General mobilized his forces and disarmed the Nuer members without any incident.

When he began arming the Dinka members surreptitiously, the suspicion of the Nuer members was aroused. They felt that something was terribly wrong and that General Marial might be up to no good. They did not feel safe and demanded that the situation be explained to them.

There was none forthcoming, so they decided to re-arm themselves for protection against the unknown. That was how the fight started within the Presidential Guard's Headquarters.

As soon as violence broke out, the initial plan to arrest the challengers of Kiir's 'executive powers' was dropped, and the incident was immediately labeled as an attempted coup.

It was a golden opportunity for Kiir! He could arrest those Political Bureau members who opposed him as coup plotters instead. He fully believed it would be a strong enough excuse to prosecute or eliminate them. This also became the reasoning used to bring forward a pogrom against Nuer civilians whose only crime was in their tribal identity.

The crux of the matter was that an attempted coup, as declared on the morning of December 16, 2013, by Salva Kiir, never existed. There was only a mutiny resulting from justified mistrust among members of Kiir's forces. Having run out of options, fabricating an attempted coup became a fortuitous way of interrupting the democratic political process by putting his political adversaries behind bars. Kiir and the coterie behind him thought that was the only avenue available to avoid the massive political defeat they were facing in the forthcoming party elections.

Nothing more! Nothing less!

CHAPTER FOUR

Salva Kiir in his Own Words and Gestures

"Our detractors say we will slip into a civil war as soon as our flag is hoisted because the concept of our democracy is faulty and that we are quick to revert to violence."

Salva Kiir Mayardit. (2011)

Criminal psychologists specializing in personalities of tyrants such as Adolf Hitler, Saddam Hussein, Joseph Stalin, Nicolae Ceausescu etc. have diagnosed them with a rare psychological condition known as a Narcissistic Personality Disorder (NPD). Like all Clinical Narcissists, Salva Kiir misrepresents facts, opportunistically shifts positions, and ignores data that conflicts with his fantasy world. He is overly confident and plays the statesman despite the overwhelming evidence that depicts him as a disaster on the political scene of South Sudan. Kiir displays a false sense of reconciliation while sublimating outward aggression.

What makes him even more dangerous is his cunning and a deceptive yet false posture of humility. Kiir suffers from the severest form of Malignant Narcissistic Personality Disorder.

As a malignant narcissist, his survival is dependent upon having control or the perception of control over all national political matters. When that control is challenged, he feels threatened and responds with brute savagery. To him, it is as though his very physical survival is at stake.

Being a control freak, Kiir has surrounded himself with codependents, enablers and a web of sycophants. However, if anyone of them challenges his authority, he simply discards that person as if he/she never existed. The victim only matters in relation to how they can support the grandiosity of the tyrant. Beyond that, they are faceless and worthless.

Paul Malong Awan and so very many of his former associates can attest to that. Salva Kiir does not have friends in the true meaning of the word found in Nilotic languages. His friends are the ones he can use to protect his power and massage his sick ego.

Kiir thinks that being a president gives one the legitimate right to kill opponents. That is why he publicly regrets sparing the lives of his erstwhile political rivals. According to Kiir, the only thing for which the South Sudanese can reward him for his contribution in the liberation struggle is the Presidency for life. To him, politics is cannibalism and 'everything goes' as long as it catches the mice for him.

After inheriting the leadership dockets upon the demise of Dr. John Garang and speaking as the Chairman of the SPLM, C-in C of the SPLA, President of the Government of Southern Sudan and the 1st Vice President of the Republic of the Sudan, in July 2005, he had this to say: "The SPLM is a vehicle without reverse gears."

With this statement, we were made to believe that when one chairman died, the next assumed the leadership to defend the gains of the revolution and deliver on the promises made to the people during the struggle.

To the dismay of so many South Sudanese and their foreign friends, none of the above transpired. What we have come to realize is that Kiir laid the SPLM vision to rest with John Garang in his Juba Mausoleum. Without a shred of shame, President Salva Kiir Mayardit returned to the cocoon of his kin and kith under the guidance of the infamous Jieng Council of Elders and has become one of the worst tribal despots in history.

Addressing the nation upon the declaration of Independence on July 9, 2011, the President called upon the citizens of South Sudan to unite behind their hard-won independence and flag. "You may be a Zande, Kakwa, Lutugo, Nuer, Dinka or Shiluk, but first remember yourself as a South Sudanese," he urged. He particularly appealed to the younger generation to refrain from tribal tendencies as nation-building requires building a national conscience. He went on to say:

> "Our detractors have already written us off even before the proclamation of independence. They say we will slip into civil war as soon as our flag is hoisted. They justify that by arguing that we are not capable of resolving our problems through dialogue. They charge that we are quick to revert to violence. They say our concept of our democracy is faulty."

While Kiir was lamenting against what he referred to as distractors, he was steering the country towards dictatorship through his one-man constitution. This would pave the way for a police state that he subsequently established in the South.

President Salva Kiir stooped low to betray everything, including his own noble historical legacy, as the only surviving heir of the founding leadership of the revolution. He betrayed those very things that earned him the right to be the First President of the Republic.

While masquerading as a statesman and a uniting beacon during his public appearances, he was recruiting a tribal private army (the earlier mentioned Dotkubeny meaning Rescue the President). Kiir was also planning to dissolve the existing SPLM Party structures, which he perceived to be threatening his authority within the Political Bureau.

The groups Kiir referred to as detractors even got it wrong when it comes to the democratic credentials of the SPLM/A. It is not even a faulty conception, as it is nonexistent. Logic has it that you can't give what you don't have. The SPLM can not give us what it does not have(democracy). In response to the Helig and Abyei crises, Kiir promised that he would not take his people back to war again. Well, who took the people back to war in the year 2013? Kiir did. This ongoing crisis of his own creation was devised purely to prolong the lifespan of his dictatorial regime.

Addressing his Dinka Community in Kuajok in November 2013 on the last leg of a tour of his home region of Bar El-Ghazal, he spoke in his mother tongue and informed them that their leadership chair ("thony dun" in Dinka) was being threatened by particular individuals in Juba and that he would count on his community to defend against that. This hate-inciting speech was well implemented by enlisting the Dinka youth in his Dotkubany parallel force, which he later commanded to massacre the Nuer.

Speaking at the Extraordinary National Convention meeting at the Nyakuron Cultural Center on Decemeber 14, 2013, Kiir alarmed and surprised the nation with his provocative words against Dr. Machar. During the speech, he promised that Machar would not be allowed to repeat what he did in 1991. The President was referring to the Dinka Bor Massacre of that year. His words were interpreted as a stark warning that those incidents would be avenged.

Holding a press conference and wearing his familiar 'tiger military fatigues on December 16, 2013, Kiir announced a state of emergency throughout South Sudan. That alarmed his colleagues. One of them quickly counseled him that he must mean curfew. Kiir quickly apologized and changed the announcement and said that he meant curfew but was confused by the linguistic difference between the two terms in Arabic and English.

Kiir then called off the state of emergency and announced dusk to dawn curfew from 6 PM to 6 AM local time in Juba. In reality, he did impose a state of emergency. It was not lifted even after the signing of the ARCSS agreement, and the arrival of the SPLM (IO) advance team in Juba on December 21, 2015.

In this press conference, Kiir described Machar as a: "prophet of doom who continues to persistently pursue his actions of the past." "However, I would like to inform you at the outset, that your government is in full control of the security situation in Juba." It goes without informing the records that the massacre of the Nuer civilians and some soldiers started immediately after he mouthed those statements. The bloodletting began at Tongpiny, Gudela, Munuki, Mangaten, and spread to 107 other areas.

Opening the Extraordinary Convention of the SPLM on January 7, 2016, the President apologized to the people of South Sudan nation for dragging them into 21 months of war. "The suffering they are going through is a result of war," Kiir said in a speech televised on the state-run SSTV. Before he finished, Kiir contradicted himself by saying that: "I will not allow cantonment in Equatoria and that any force that claims to be IO there will be hunted down like rats." This was a precursor to the heinous atrocities throughout that region that year.

Launching his National Dialogue project in October 2017, the President had this to say: "In the spirit of national unity, forgiveness, and dialogue I am asking you, the people of South Sudan, to forgive me for any mistakes I might have committed during my tenure as your leader. This is the spirit that our country needs, and we must act now." While he was saying this, he was launching a scorched earth offensive on the SPLM/A (IO) positions in the country and committing atrocities against the civilian population.

Addressing the Dinka Agar community in Rumbek on July 14, 2014, Kiir launched a very inciting appeal to stop their infighting and unite to confront t the common enemy (the Nuer). He also referred to himself as a tiger whose claws were now out and prepared for a bloodbath in this country. He said those who mess with him now mess with an agitated tiger.

Challenged by Stephen Sucker of BBC Hard Talk in a face-to-face interview about the plight of the people in UNMISS, Kiir said those Nuer in POCS are all rebels who are lucky to even be alive. He then stated that many Dinka people in the Upper Nile states did not survived like they did here in Juba.

On July 30, 2015, Kiir publicly revealed reason behind the creation of 28 states by declaring that the oil fields in Unity and Falosh belonged to the Dinka community. The imaginary maps of his new tribal states have created a permanent conflict among the communities who have lived without borders since time immemorial.

In a VOA radio interview, Kiir said reports about the refugee situation were overblown and the people had fled because they were "told to by social media." Asked about the death of the American journalist his forces labeled as a white rebel, the President said an American news photographer, killed by government troops in August, was "fighting on behalf of the rebels."

Just like his cowboy hat, Kiir's trademark is political violence. His fascist regime has been killing journalists, raping and killing aid workers as a means to deny humanitarian access to the opposition-controlled areas since July 2016. There is no crime under the sun that Kiir's regime has not committed during this crisis. The regime has gone as practicing state terrorism by kidnapping journalists and civil society activists in neighboring countries.

Adding to the ongoing orgy of genocide, Kiir has discovered another way to kill. He did so by creating famine in the Southern Unity State constituency of Dr. Machar through violent displacement.

As well documented in the AU Commission of Inquiry Report, it was Kiir who fabricated a coup as a ploy to eliminate his opponents in December 2013 and committed genocide against ethnic Nuers in the process.

According to the findings of the UN Panel of Experts report, it was Kiir who reintroduced violence by attempting to murder Dr.Machar who was then his First President in violation of the ARCSS agreement in July 2016. This resulted in returning the country to virulent bloodletting.

Presently, South Sudan under Salva Kiir is known on the world map for nothing but war, corruption, genocide, famine and a never-ending refugee and humanitarian crisis.

Our downtrodden people have been plunged into a bottom-less pit of death and destruction. Lives and properties have been destroyed in a scale and we have never seen. More than during the two decades of war with the Republic of Sudan. Worse yet, this terrible war has wrecked the social fabric of our society beyond description.

In sum, it is a history of a failed state, systematic genocide, civil war, famine, intra-communal violence, institutionalized corruption, economic crisis, and mass trauma. The question lingering in so many minds is: What has gone so very wrong to turn us into this pathological society of murderers?

You may do all the diagnoses modern science can come up with and end up with empirical findings that violence is not predisposed in our DNA. Our predicament is squarely that of total leadership failure in the person of none other than our inept accidental President.

While criticizing late Dr. John Garang at the Rumbek meeting in 2004 on the failures of SPLM/A leadership to fight rampant corruption within the rank and files of the army, Salva Kiir lamented: "SPLA members have formed private companies, bought houses and have huge bank accounts in foreign countries. I wonder what kind of system we are going to establish in South Sudan?"

That was a valid question. However, what type of system do we have now under Salva Kiir? It is graft formulated and led by none other than himself. Kiir continues to bash everyone around him for corruption, but the bitter truth is that he is the lead agent of this foul practice in South Sudan today. As evidently verified by the fact that his J1 Palace has been scandalized by domestic grand theft, President is the center of that graft.

His own his Press Man,Ateny Wek Ateny revealed lately that General Paul Malong, Salva Kiir, and his palace cabal have converted J1 into a secret branch of the South Sudan Central Bank opened only at night for blody businesses and kleptomania. Kiir accuses his own aides of theft and then promotes them to higher dockets with greater access to state coffers to advance and perfect their graft.

The case in point is that of his former Chief Administrator, Mayen Wol, who was appointed the Undersecretary in the Ministry of Petroleum upon his release from jail without trial for theft and embezzlement of public funds in J1.

It has become an open secret in South Sudan that the regime has lagged behind in paying the salaries of its civil servants for years. This is simply because the bulk of our national budget, funded with petrodollars, goes to Kiir's war machine and his fat bank accounts abroad. The rest goes into the pockets of his hoodlums guarding the throne. This has been verified and confirmed by credible inter-national financial intelligence. That is why the United States government has imposed sanctions on the financial institutions and the private businesses of the regime's top graft-lords including the President himself.

Like all dictators in world history, Kiir cannot survive and thrive without conflict as it is the conflict itself that keeps him in power and offer him the opportunity to loot and kill with impunity. Knowing very well that peace might end him along with the of war he created, he is admannt to do everything possible to invent more ways to prolong the war as a means to extend the lifespan of his rogue regime.

Addressing a huge gathering of jubilant citizens gathered at the Juba International Airport to receive a peace message from him, Kiir drove his captive audience to desolation when he pressed home a very negative message. He accused the rebels of violating the ceasefire by attacking the government positions in Equatoria and Western Bahr El Ghazal. Quite a statement when the whole world was very well informed that it was his government that has always been on the offensive. In a very threatening tone, he told the crowd that: "I can crush the rebels right now if I order my generals to rout them from their hideouts in the countryside."

A very discouraging gesture was made with the presidential amnesty he offered to Dr. Machar and all of those he called 'rebels' on August 8, 2018. The entire opposition block and the mediators saw that as a mockery to the spirit of the recently signed 'CoH' and the permanent ceasefire. One which his regime had been violating since December 2017.

Speaking in a mix of English and SPLA Arabic, the President went on to dwell on the absurd and divisive story of his Khartoum encounter with a Dinka rebels whom he ridiculed for killing the Dinka fighting for General Thomas Cirilo, a man who was in charge of killing the Dinka.

Kiir stooped even lower by blasting the Dinka Bor community, where the Dinka rebel Commander Ayuen hails from, by reminding them that their cattle are responsible for the ongoing conflict between Equatorians and the Dinka government in that region. He went on to say: "We the Bahr El Ghazalians do not bring our cows here to cause trouble in Equatoria." This was directed at General Jok Riak, his Chief of Staff from Bor, who was in attendance.

I think the tribal bigot forgot in that absurd utterance about his own herd of cows in Luri. His petty tribal talk dejected the masses in South Sudan who thought their President was returning home with peace at hand. His body language demonstrated that he had not reconciled with the opposition. This sent a desolate shockwave across those parts of the world that cared about South Sudan and was spread via the social media. This hateful speech was full of polemic, gimmicks and unnecessary threats. The whole thing was extremely divisive and politically poisonous to the peace process.

Evidently, Salva Kiir thrives on boxing the people of South Sudan into Jieng, Naath, Bari, Bor Jieng, Bar Elghazalians and so forth. Divide and conquer. Over the five-year span of this latest crisis, he has transformed the conflict into permanent all out intra-tribal warfare. In the process, he mobilized every ethnic community against the Jieng.

President Kiir's counter-insurgency tactics are also dangerous as they are geared toward pitting communities against one another in Greater Upper Nile. His project of fueling Murle-Dinka Bor intra-communal violence by supplying both communities with lethal weapons is the hallmark of that deadly policy. Kiir's Machiavellian administration and divisive local politics have caused even more deaths in his own Jieng communities of the Lakes and Warrap states where inter-communal violence has claimed thousands of lives since 2005. South Sudan is now fully developed in the image of Salva Kiir. It is violent, corrupt, politically incompetent and ethnically polarized. He has squandered all the goodwill from his legacy as a veteran of the liberation struggle. In sum his leadership produced the following vices:

- Rampant Corruption that has now developed into a kleptocratic state.
- Institutionalized Tribalism that has now evolved into an ethno-centric state.
- Rampant insecurity that has evolved to genocide, mass displace-

ment, and a refugee crisis.

- Underachieving social and economic development despite oil money resulting in total economic collapse.
- A constitutional crisis that that has resulted in a military dicta-torship/police state.
- A loss of vision and ideological direction within the ruling SPLM Party that has resulted in a split of the party into many factions.
- Poor international relations that relegated South Sudan to a 'pariah regime' status.

All of the above crises provide conclusive evidence that President Salva Kiir is miserably ill-equipped to govern and rule. His country's history will list him only as the First President of the Republic. In all fairness, history of South Sudan will remember President Kiir only for the following spectacularly silly things: His trademark(giant black hat) which presents him as a cowboy clown, contro-versial presidential decrees, redundant speeches, his politically immature outbursts as recorded in the footnotes below,instigating crises, pardoning criminals and rewarding them with high posts to protect his power, economic crisis,institutionalized corruption and political tribalism during of his tyrannical and violence' tenure.

The history of South Sudan must also record that the state under Salva Kiir was repressive and highly oppressive. This means that, there was no freely expressed plurality of political views during his reign of terror and public insecurity. Domestic and international journalists were intimidated, harassed, arrested, or expelled. Many media facilities were closed or operated with shackles. In addition to all this, he pushed the nascent nation to the precipice of implo-sion, destruction, and insolvency.

"Those Nuers at UNMISS camps in Juba are even lucky to be

alive in those fences. The Dinka in Upper Nile were all killed"
Salva Kiir Mayardit. (2014)

"Where do I get the national army to execute the war when Riek Machar took his Nuers to the bush with him and Wani Iga cannot prevent his Equatorian sons from joining Riek Machar in the bush? I have to use my Dinka boys to defend my government."
Salva Kiir Mayardit. (2017)

"The Social media displaced the people, but it is not a big deal. The humanitarian organizations will come back and serve the people."
Kiir (2017).

"They want me to sign peace & replace me but where is my incentive if I sign that peace?"
Salva Kiir Mayardit (December 2017)

"I regret even sparing lives of those FDS, Riek Machar and Paul Malong"
Salva Kiir Mayardit, *Sudan Tribune* (May 2, 2018);

CHAPTER FIVE

The IGAD Initiative of December 2013

Phase I

The twenty-month peace process to resolve the crisis in South Sudan was an initiative of the IGAD Heads of State. As a member of this regional bloc, they had the consent and membership of the Government of the Republic of South Sudan.

The initiative was taken within two weeks of the onset of the crisis. The regional leaders conducted intensive shuttle diplomacy between Juba and Gadiang, the then headquarters of the SPLM/A, to expeditiously avert the looming civil war. That culminated in the 23rd Extraordinary Session of the IGAD Assembly of the Head of States and Governments on December 27, 2013, at State House in Nairobi, Kenya. It was headed by Desalegn Haile Mariem, the Prime Minister of Ethiopia and the then Chairman of IGAD.

In attendance were: Ismail Omar Guelleh, President of the Republic of Djibouti, Uhuru Kenyatta, President of the Republic of Kenya, Hassan Sheikh Mohamud, President of the Federal Republic of Somalia, Yoweri Kaguta Museveni, President of the Republic of Uganda, Bakri Hassan Saleh, First Vice President of the Republic of the Sudan and Dr. Barnaba Marial Benjamin, Minister of Foreign Affairs of South Sudan. H.E. Ambassador Mahboub Maalim, the Executive Secretary of IGAD and Ambassador Erastus Mwencha, Deputy Chairperson of the African Union Commission.

The session received a briefing from the Chair of the IGAD Council of Ministers and the Minister of Foreign Affairs of Ethiopia,

H.E. Tedros Adhanom on an emergency three-day visit to Juba on December 19, 2013. The content of the briefing was the overall report on the political and security situation in South Sudan.

The regional leaders came up with the first communiqué intended to resolve the conflict. Article 15 of that communiqué underlined the importance of the following:

▌ To welcome the commitment of the Government of South Sudan to enact cessation of hostilities and unconditionally begin dialogue with the armed opposition and all stakeholders in the country.

▌ Urged the Government of South Sudan to ensure protection for civilians, humanitarian workers and citizens of the neighboring countries doing business in the country.

▌ Strongly condemn the criminal acts of murder, sexual violence, looting and other criminal acts against civilians and unarmed combatants by any party and demand that all involved be held responsible by their de facto and or de jure leaders.

▌ To undertake urgent measures in pursuit of an all-inclusive dialogue including reviewing the status of the political detainees in recognition of their role in accordance with the law of the Republic of South Sudan and in creating a conducive environment for all stakeholders to participate and determine that face-to-face talks by all stakeholders in the conflict should take place by December 31, 2013.

The meeting directed the IGAD Council of Ministers to continue working with the Government of South Sudan and to initiate contact with Dr. Riek Machar and other leaders critical to bringing about peace and to keep the summit apprised of the situation.

The extraordinary session also urged the United Nations to support the IGAD led peace process in South Sudan to ensure humanitarian assistance and to support constitutional and other political reforms in South Sudan.

Finally, the session authorized the IGAD Secretariat to organize peace talks between the South Sudanese warring parties to take place in Addis Ababa, Ethiopia. The communiqué also authorized the head of IGAD member states minus South Sudan and Uganda to appoint special envoys to serve as the mediating body at the talks.

In response to that, the Democratic Federal Republic of Ethiopia then appointed Ambassador Seyoum Mesfin, the former Ethiopian Minister of Foreign Affairs. Sudan appointed General Mohamed Ahmed Aldabi, the former Ambassador and professional intelligence officer in the Sudanese Army. Kenya appointed General Lazaro Sumbeiywo, a retired army general who brokered the Comprehensive Peace Agreement (CPA) between the then Sudan People's Liberation Army and the Government of the Republic of Sudan and Mahboub Maalim of Djibouti.

The Secretariat, composed of those special envoys from the four IGAD member states, sent letters of invitation to the heads of the warring parties to send their delegations to Addis Ababa for talks. The parties responded promptly by sending delegations to the Ethiopian capital. The first session of the peace talks then took place at the Sheraton Hotel in Addis Ababa on January 4, 2014. The IGAD mediation team framed the agenda on January 6, 2014, as follows:

▌ Discussion and adoption of the draft modalities of South Sudan Dialogue.
▌ Discussion and adoption of the draft rules of procedures for the dialogue.
▌ Adoption of the draft structure and Terms of References (TOR).

The mediation designed peace process was to progress in phases: Phase I was about stopping the bloodletting and Phase II was about addressing the root causes of the conflict. The first round of Phase I was concluded with the Cessation of Hostility Agreement (COHA), signed on January 23, 2014, between the two warring parties. It included the following basic provisions:

- Immediate cessation of all offensive military operations and avoidance of any action that could provoke military confrontation between the two combatant forces.
- Both parties were to refrain from targeting unarmed and non-combatant civilians.
- Both parties were to mutually refrain from any action that may damage national installations including oil fields.
- Allow free and safe access to humanitarian assistance for the civil population in combatant zones.
- Permit free travel of the VMT (Verification and Monitoring Team) which includes personnel and aircraft from IGAD, AU, Norway, the UK, and the US.
- Take immediate action to ensure that any location taken by any party in violation of COH is immediately restored to the party that had control over those areas prior to the violation.
- The parties shall communicate the COH to their respective commands for observation and implementation.
- Immediate compliance and cooperation with the COH and VMT.

In sum, the agreement was the commitment to cease all military action aimed at each other and any other action that may undermine the peace process upon signing. This meant the cessation of all military operations and the forces were to be frozen in their current locations. All parties to the agreement were to refrain from taking any action that could invite military confrontation. This included all movements of forces, ammunition resupply, or any other action that could be viewed as confrontational. The parties further agreed to ensure that all forces or armed groups under their influence, control and/or command shall observe the terms of the agreement.

CHAPTER SIX

Phase II:
The Tone and Tune
of the Talks at the Peace Table

"Real peace means the one that guarantees the present and makes the future bright, prosperous and possible, and throws away the specter of war and violence"

Stella Gait.ano

The IGAD initiative found me in Kampala, Uganda where I joined my family for Christmas after escaping the genocide in Juba. It angered and saddened me greatly that my closest bodyguard, Sergeant Major Nai Gai, was killed in the pogrom targeting Nuers in the national capital. Consequently, I decided to resign my post in Jonglei State as the Minister of Education. However, my family and friends, particularly Abraham Keat and James Maluit, advised me to wait for the dust to settle before making major decisions.

Only my cousin, Colonel Gai Chatiem Pouch, serving as the Defense Attaché at the South Sudan Embassy in Kampala encouraged me to resign and keep writing against the genocidal regime.

While contemplating tendering of my resignation, I could not help writing two articles. One was entitled *South Sudan: Another Rwanda in the Making* and the other one was entitled *The Fingerprints on Genocide in South Sudan*. The prior was published while I was still in Juba and that put my life in danger. The later was published while I was in Kampala.

Upon reading my critical articles, Governor John Kong, who did not want me to continue in his government, decreed me out with the other ministers who rebelled along with me. They were: Hussein Mar Nyuot, Commissioner Goi Jok Yul, Gabriel Duop Lam, and Manawa Peter Gatkuoth.

While in Nairobi, I and my good friend Dei Tut Weang in collaboration with other comrades started organizing as a cell and reported to Dr. Machar in Gadiang.

Out of this came an initiative. Dr. Machar, then composed the peace delegation under a tree in Gatdiang and put me and Dr. Dhiew Mathuok who had just joined us in the list We then flew overnight on Ethiopian Airlines to Bole International Airport in Addis Ababa via Kigali International Airport in the Republic of Rwanda on January 6, 2014. We joined our comrades the following morning.

The SPLM/A delegation led by Governor Taban Deng was a bulky one. It was comprised of so many disgruntled members of the infant movement coming from Juba, the neighboring countries, and the Diaspora. Only Cde Goi Jok Yul and Cde Taban Deng came from Gadiang.

The Government delegation led by Nhial Deng Nhial was also large. It was comprised of members of the SPLM (IG) and two veteran politicians from other parties in the government, Dr. Lam Akol of the SPLM-DC and Ustaz Joseph Ukel of USUP.

The first encounter between the two delegations was emotional and volatile. It was war talk, not peace talk. Despite the adoption of the rules of engagement which warned against the blame game and finger pointing, the first exchanges were verbally confrontational.

One of the most contentious issues was the name and the political identity of the armed opposition which insisted on calling itself the SPLM/A. Peter Bisher Bendy and Michael Makuei Lueth of the government delegation were particularly dismissive of that, saying that there is no way Riek Machar's group can call itself something that would contradict the status of the SPLM/A in the Government.

In response to their dismissive attitude, we insisted that the SPLM in the Government could neither dismiss our identity as SPLM nor name us in the process of this dialogue. Then came the question regarding whether the talks were actually between the Government and the armed opposition or between the two SPLM factions (one in the government and the other in opposition). That question took the parties to the root causes of the conflict, which in fact originated from within the then united ruling SPLM Party. The mediators then reached the conclusion that the dialogue was essentially between the two factions of the SPLM.

That angered members of other parties in the government delegation who maintained that what they were in was a government delegation, not the SPLM Party's delegation per se. That put mediation at loggerheads. However, it was decided to use their own working language to name the parties and the mediators announced the decision in the afternoon session. From that point on, the opposition was to be known as SPLM/A - In Opposition or SPLA (IO) and the other delegation was to be called GRSS (Government of the Republic of South Sudan). That is how the name we are using today came into being. That at least put each party at ease to continue with the dialogue. However, the chemistry between the parties was still volatile and emotional.

The afternoon session was particularly hot and confrontational. The opposition came up with testimonies of genocide by the government and the government delegation dwelt heavily on the coup narrative. We called each other names like genocidaire, dictators, rebels and coup-plotters. The mediators allowed us to breathe out all that fire but advised that armed confrontation on the ground, name-calling at the table, and blame games would not resolve the conflict.

Nevertheless the negative tone continued throughout the first phase. The government side was particularly sarcastic and dismissive. As opined in Nhial Deng's opening speech, Kiir's regime was gearing more for war than peace. Although the opposition was playing as a victim of dictatorship and genocide, it was also gearing for armed resistance and actions that could possibly oust Kiir's regime militarily.

The White Army was still advancing toward Juba as the talks were in progress. The official political position of the IO was that Kiir must go and that he must give way to a transitional government that could take the people of South Sudan to elections. Otherwise, the war would continue.

General Taban Deng, the SPLM/A (IO) Chief Negotiator, was far more diplomatic than Nhial Deng Nhial (GRSS), who sounded bombastic and confrontational throughout his speech. In his opening statement, General Deng thanked the regional and international leadership for charting the path toward peace in South Sudan. He then presented the official position of the SPLM/A (IO) in the form of the following demands:

- The release of all the political detainees and to accord them the political space to join the peace process.
- Total withdrawal of Ugandan troops and all other foreign forces in the country.
- Lifting the State of Emergency throughout the country.
- Afford humanitarian access to the IDPs in the UNMISS camps throughout the country.
- Give free access to the UNHCR and other international human rights organizations to investigate war crimes and the ongoing genocide in the country.

▌ Affirmed the SPLM/IO commitment to the IGAD mediation.

The government rejected all that as mere advancement of what they called the 'coup agenda'. In his long speech, Nhial Deng dwelt on that narrative in a futile attempt to create an impression in the minds of the envoys and the international observers present. He stated that the root cause of the crisis was a failed coup attempt by the leadership of the armed opposition and their allies under detention in Juba.

In his sarcastic presentation, Nhial offered nothing other than a permanent ceasefire and presidential amnesty for what he called the failed coup-makers and all the rebels carrying arms against the elected Government of the Republic of South Sudan. Judging from his body language in the opening session, he appeared to be a demagogue and propagandist.

This view came out very clearly in the opening speeches of TROIKA and the European Union envoys. They made strongly worded presentations demanding negotiations in good faith to reform the institutions of the South Sudan Government that mismanaged the crisis. They further warned the warring parties of swift action if the parties failed to reach a peaceful agreement sooner than later!

The EU and the British envoy strongly cautioned the Government of the Republic of South Sudan to curb the escalation of violence against unarmed civilians in the country. They also warned them of severe criminal justice measures against the perpetrators of those brutal acts against civilians, women, and children in South Sudan.

This was very much in line with the IGAD Communiqué issued out of the 23rd Extraordinary Session.

The regime continued to chase the coup story that had long been dismissed by the region and the international community at the commencement of talks. Another thing Kiir's delegation of highly learned and experienced negotiators failed to grasp, was that the armed opposition and their colleagues in detention were already recognized as victims of Salva Kiir's tyranny.

Dr. Lam later told me privately that the opposition was scoring high in the diplomatic front. Coming from a diplomat and politician of his caliber, I took that seriously. Nevertheless, Nhial and Kiir's cronies continued to defy international pressure to negotiate in good faith.

As the talks were going on, Kiir's regime advanced on the Juba-Bor Road recapturing Bor and threatening our headquarters in Gadiang. This was aided by the Ugandan Air Force's use of cluster bombs to deter the White Army. As a result, Kiir's delegation in Addis rapidly cranked up the volume on 'war talk'.

My cousin and close friend General Thomas Duoth Guet of Kiir's External Security approached me with mocking advice to accept a permanent ceasefire before the rebellion was militarily crushed. That I saw as an insult to my movement. I was very angry but hid my feelings and managed to mildly tell him that he should know better as a former guerrilla soldier. Offering us permanent ceasefire and presidential amnesty is a polite way of demanding surrender to Kiir's whims. I then cautioned him to respect our personal relationship as relatives and friends who did so many things together in the past. We ended in a positive way with vows that we would compare notes in the near future.

True, they were militarily advancing, but crushing a guerrilla movement with a strong community support base like ours was farfetched, in my humble opinion.

The first round of talks failed to achieve anything more than the two agreements. One on the release of Political detainees and the Cessation of Hostility Agreement (COH). The latter was never implemented despite the formation of a Verification and Monitoring Team (VMT). The release of political detainees did materialize partially through President Uhuru Kenyatta's personal diplomacy and from pressure internationally.

Otherwise, from the outset, the South Sudanese Peace Talks in Addis Ababa were forums of verbal savagery and combative political polemics throughout. That was why theey collapsed without agreement several times over 20 months.

The two delegations were simply not engaging in meaningful peace negotiations. Peacemaking takes trust and respect between the protagonists. They must respect one another in their leadership positions and what they represent. In our case as the opposition, we perceived the delegation of Kiir's regime as a bunch of killers who must pay for the crimes they committed against the people of South Sudan. To the Kiir delegation, we were a bevy of power-hungry opportunists who had committed treason by attempting to overthrow a democratically elected government and wanted to use the death of the people to ascend to power.

In a very provocative tone, Honorable Michael Makuei Lueth, the Minister of Information and the Spokesman for the government delegation kept calling the SPLM (IO) delegation rebels delegation instead of referring to us as the 'opposition' as stipulated in the ground rules of conduct.

It was openly evident that there was no chemistry between the two delegations. Nhial Deng and Taban Deng, the sons of Deng as some called them, tried to forge understanding. Alas, they were quickly accused by hardliners on both sides of colluding against their bosses for a double regime change to replace both Kiir and Machar.

I can vividly recall that the mood was prevalently that of war and conflict. The delegations that were expected to bring peace were fighting and aggravating the situation. The government delegation was counting on their military victories on the ground to dictate the terms at the table.

The delegation of SPLM/A (IO), formed spontaneously in response to the Juba massacre of the Nuer in mid-December 2013, came to the talks with memories of this still fresh in their minds.

To us, any peace agreement that leaves Kiir at the helm amounts to a betrayal of our brethren butchered in cold blood.

One thing I realized later was that the talk of genocide has a deep impact on our collective attitude toward peace. Hence, the peacemaking process became war-making at the table. The victimology of this genocidal war mentally framed the dichotomy of the conflict as innocent victims versus vicious perpetrators. But what is the value of clinical binaries when each party can speak the language of victimhood? The Government maintained victimhood by calling us as coup planners. We maintained victimhood by virtue of being the survivors of Juba's pogrom.

Michael Makuei uttered in one of the plenary sessions: "Fighting negative forces does not amount to genocide." Although some of the hardliners in our delegation did not like embracing the language of victimhood, that statement by Michael Makuei provoked extreme anger among them. That pushed many of us to the extreme to rather express only their willingness and ability to rid South Sudan of Kiir's genocidal regime. This also provoked major fear and anger among the Jieng extremists like Madam Awut Deng, Martin Majut Yak, Makuei Lueth and others in the government delegation.

So, the tone and the tune of the negotiations were dominated by a shared fear and implied promises of mutual destruction. Those of us who lacked peace negotiation experience approached it like a court case where we expected the mediators to issue a verdict. In fact, they did so with the 'take or leave it' approach in the form of the compromised draft agreement. This became known as The Agreement on the Resolution of the Conflict in South Sudan (ARCSS). In general, none of the protagonists ever negotiated in good faith to make genuine concessions or address the fundamental root causes of the conflict.

Conventionally, peace can be built by collectively acknowledging and appreciating the differences that caused the conflict at hand and to use those differences positively in order to resolve said conflict. In other words, if the conflict is about the differences, then peace comes only through addressing those differences.

That was not the case in Addis Ababa. For one thing, there is no culture of dialogue in the ruling SPLM/A. We only have had a culture of war and political violence. The mediators demanded mutual respect to facilitate the dialogue, but all in vain. The finger-pointing and counter-accusations continued throughout. The war talk continued to rage both in Pagak and Juba. The government delegation always came with instructions to make no concessions that could later empower Riek Machar to gain control of the government.

In Pagak, all the consultative leadership meetings directed the peace delegation to maintain the SPLM (IO) position that there would be no peace or return to Juba with Kiir in power.

The second leadership meeting of the SPLM/A (IO) convened in Pagak on April 23, 2015 declared that the term of South Sudan Parliament and the presidency expired the previous month on March 8. The meeting further urged the region and the international community to declare Salva Kiir illegitimate.

The question then was: How do you exclude Kiir from power without decisive military victory in the battlefield? The implied gesture in my humble view was protracted armed struggle.

From the Radison Blue Hotel in Addis to Debre Zeit, Bahir Dar, The Capital Hotel and ECA building, the thematic committee rarely agreed on any tangible thing. The position of the government has always been about limited power sharing at the center, absorption of the SPLA (IO) forces within three months and a return to the status quo.

Evidently, Kiir's regime was using the dialogue as a public relations exercise. They were in Addis Ababa to buy time while they continued to toil for a military solution on the ground. In what looked like a monologue with the deaf, they proposed that it was up to the opposition as the aggrieved party to make presentations and that the government's job was to react to those presentations.

This non-dialogical approach was designed to waste time and frustrate the entire process. However, we acted in good faith and proceeded as agreed upon. From the political framework to the rainbow document, the opposition made elaborate presentations on all areas of needed reforms in Kiir's dysfunctional system.

On structural and institutional reforms, we made the case for the need to overhaul the current civil service and the public security sector currently dominated by Kiir's clan. At the constitutional level, we exposed the decay of the regime by pointing out that the two main branches of Kiir's government (judiciary and executive) were made dockets of Kiir's home state.

To entrench and institutionalize their kleptocracy, they also took control of the Treasury (both Finance and the Central Bank). This depicted Kiir's clannish oligarchy as a criminal establishment that must be dismantled to form an inclusive national government.

On governance and the system of government, we made the case for an amendment of the existing one-man's constitution to implement a fully-fledged federal system. In response, Kiir's delegation acknowledged that federalism is a historical and political demand of the people of South Sudan but maintained without elaboration that the time to address it was not now.

On the demobilization of irregular forces and formation of a new army, they maintained that their political status as a legitimate government granted them the right to recruit from their ethnic states of Warrap and Northern Bahr-El Ghazal.

In sum, the opposition forces and other stakeholders made the case for institutional reforms, democratic transformation, peace, reconciliation and accountability for war crimes committed by both

sides of the armed conflict. Kiir's delegation dismissed all the grievances and drove home the point that they would not allow anything
that tampers with the status quo. To them, meaningful power-
sharing with other parties for a democratic transition leading to free
and fair elections meant outright regime change and the ouster of
Salva Kiir. That is very clear from the language of their responses,
which were heavily weighted regarding the legitimacy and sovereignty of South Sudan.

From what we have heard throughout the talks, Kiir and
company arrogated the sovereignty of South Sudan to themselves
as their sole possession. According to them, legitimacy and sovereignty gave them all the rights including the right to amend the
existing transitional constitution to indefinitely cling on to their
dictatorial power. It became very evident that 'rule of guns' attitude
that Kiir and his cronies used to obstruct the democratic process
and commit mass homicide in December 2013, was not deterred. It
was well represented at the table by Kiir's arrogant team of negotiators. Nhial Deng Nhial, the Chief Negotiator of the regime did
every thing to intellectually bully the SPLM(IO) Chief Negotiator,
General Taban Deng Gai.

We were always there to take the pain of Nhial Deng's eloquent
blusters, Makuei Lueth's sarcastic outbursts, and Kok Ruei's
thunderous tantrums.

Kiir's delegation had never gone to Addis Ababa in a genuine
search for peace as they were counting on military victory in the
field. Anything other than a permanent ceasefire and re-integration
of opposition forces into their tribal army (Mathiang Anyor) within
three months was deferred to what they called a National Dialogue
in Juba.

They also stated that the opposition should represent only those
areas under their military control. The mediators and the stakeholders present heard that loud and clear as a negotiation of victors

versus the vanquished. The rest of the points were contemptuous gestures against the opposition parties (whether armed or not), civil society organizations and the clergy. It was a militaristic attitude that tends to push all to a protracted armed struggle. Otherwise, one can conclude with ease that the regime lost the political debate in Addis Ababa. The only song they kept sing ing, with rhyming lyrics was their stollen legitimacy.

What they deliberately ignored was the cold truth that it is the people who conferred legitimacy upon them and it is never a divine entitlement. It follows that the same people who conferred it must be able to revoke it. Conventional practice teaches us that it is not the election per se that sustains legitimacy, but how the elected political leader in question governs.

From the Radisson Blue Hotel to Bahir Dar and the United Nations Economic Commission building in Addis Ababa, the talks continued regarding institutional reforms, the system of governance, power-sharing, transitional security arrangements, transitional justice, permanent constitution-making, and elections. The FDs and SPLM (IO) made presentations and the Government delegation, dubbed as the SPLM (IG), responded either contemptuously or fallaciously.

We defined the predicament of South Sudan as a leadership crisis in the person of General Salva Kiir with the following manifestations:

- Lack of respect for human rights and the rule of law.
- Lack of political space for freedom of expression.
- Censorship of public and private media.
- Domination of the national army, police, organized forces, and security organs by one ethnic group.

This was elaborated by highlighting that the two tiers of the government (Executive and Judiciary) had been allotted to Warrap, the home state of the President. The President had also converted the South Sudan National Assembly into his rubber stamp.

▊ Politicization of the civil service and the security sector. Kiir appointed all the director generals in the national ministries. All senior civil servants have become political appointees of the president.
▊ A dysfunctional judicial system where the courts are rendered useless.
▊ A lack of internal democracy in the ruling SPLM Party.
▊ A lack of checks and balances in the three pillars of government whereas the legislature becomes an extension of the President.

That was and is still the truth. However, hearing it all fanned the bitter and boiling tempers within the Government delegation. This was somewhat moderated in Bahar Dar but the power-sharing discussion was never easy. The war talks attitude came back in a major way upon return to Addis Ababa. This widened the gap further. The mediators were always there to take note of our highly conflicting and emotionally charged presentations both in a proxy format and in thematic committee meetings.

The gap remained wide with the following opposing negotiating positions on power-sharing:

▊ The SPLM (IG) proposed the maintenance of the status quo with President Salva Kiir as Head of State and Government, VP Wani as the First Vice President and an accommodation of the SPLM (IO) in the position of the Second Vice President. This could be Riek Machar or his nominee. There would be an allocation of 80% of power to the GRSS and 20% of power to be shared by the SPLM (IO), SPLM (FPD), other political parties, etc.

- The SPLM (IO) proposed the size of the cabinet be 31 ministers with the President and one VP to lead the transition and that the President must come from the SPLM (IO). They would allocate 70% of power to themselves leaving the rest to share 30%.
- The other political parties proposed President Kiir to be the incumbent and the VP would be from the SPLM (IO)
- The parties agreed to share power but failed to reach an agreement on the power-sharing percentages and allocations. The talks then collapsed as usual.

Declaration of Principles (DOPS)

As a prelude to the commencement of the talks, the mediation came up with a declaration of principles roadmap entitled: Toward Peace, Reconciliation, and Accountability. The documents declared the cardinal principles of the talks as follows:

- To negotiate in good faith for a win-win solution guided by national interest and adhering to the full implementation of agreements reached to resolve the current crisis.
- To acknowledge that political power emanates from the people and therefore:
- To permanently renounce violence and unconstitutional means of taking over power that undermines the sovereignty of the People of South Sudan.
- To strongly reject the ideology and politics of negative ethnicity and other forms of sectarianism.
- To agree and commit themselves to a peaceful transfer of power through democratic and peaceful means in accordance with the constitution of the country.

▌ To fully accept and commit themselves to the idea that there is no military solution to the conflict, and that a peaceful, just and inclusive political solution must be the common objective of all South Sudanese.

▌ To commit to a negotiated settlement and to implement all agreements reached by the parties in the political negotiations towards National Reconciliation and Healing, and those agreements shall be enshrined in the constitution.

▌ Acknowledge the diversity of the people of South Sudan and reaffirm the country's unity in diversity and territorial integrity.

▌ Ensure that the political and social equality of all the people of South Sudan is guaranteed by law.

▌ Strengthen good governance, democratic principles, justice, accountability, transparency, and fundamental human rights and freedoms; and to engage in essential constitutional, legal and institutional reforms.

▌ Adhere to internationally accepted humanitarian principles and unhindered humanitarian access to all areas affected by the conflict.

▌ Safety and security is the right of all citizens of South Sudan, and the review and reorganization of national security institutions shall be undertaken with a view to instilling professionalism and reforms including equitable representation, strengthened by broad, accountable and transparent validation.

▌ Protect human lives and public and private property including key installations and the national infrastructure.

▌ The national wealth belongs to all citizens of South Sudan. The financial welfare and macroeconomic stability of the country shall thus be safeguarded in a transparent and equitable manner so as to meet the needs and development aspirations of all its citizens.

▌ Agree that participants to an all-inclusive National Political Dialogue Conference towards sustainable peace, national reconciliation and healing shall include but not be limited to the following: Political parties, eminent personalities, women, youth and faith-based organizations, people with special needs, traditional leaders, war widows, veterans and the war wounded, business leaders, trade unions, professional associations and the academia. A conference shall be held after the parties have reached final agreement on all issues underlying current armed conflict.

▮ Political dialogue shall aim at finding immediate solutions to the crisis through the following:

▮ Adopting immediate solutions and measures to address the appalling humanitarian needs, restoring peace, reconciliation, national healing, confidence, and harmony in order to return the country to normalcy.

▮ An all-inclusive National Political Dialogue Conference shall find long-term solutions to the issues of the system of governance, democracy, human rights, justice, national unity, cohesion and integration, security, development and wealth management.

The Quest for Inclusivity

The Addis Ababa talks started as a dialogue between the two SPLM factions. However, as they progressed there emerged a massive demand for inclusivity from the friends of IGAD and other parties beginning in January 2014. Thanks to the intensive diplomacy of the former detainees (SPLM-FDS) and civil society organizations, the SPLM (IO) was the first to respond in acceptance of that demand.

The government initially rejected the whole notion of multi-party talks or multi-stakeholder talks. However, with pressure from mediation and the friends of IGAD, TROIKA and the EU, the government agreed to the process.

To identify the participants, a symposium was organized to take place on June 7, 2014 in Addis Ababa. The multi-stakeholder event was held to initiate an inclusive phase of the peace process. It was successful and concluded at the United Nations Economic Commission Conference Center. More than 250 South Sudanese representing the government, the opposition, political parties, faith-based groups, and civil society organizations participated in the two-day gathering.

During the symposium, renowned international experts offered overview presentations in key thematic areas, including transitional governance arrangements and interim institutions, justice, reconciliation, and healing, security arrangements and constitutional development and reform.

Later on, the participants informally explored and discussed the issues with subject matter experts in order to further advance their understanding and the concepts. The IGAD Special Envoy General, Lazaro Sumbeiywo, who chaired the two-day deliberations, explained that the meeting was not a platform for negotiations, but would serve as a forum to educate, inform and to share knowledge and experiences with the participants.

Giving the keynote speech at the beginning of the symposium, H.E. Dr. Tedros Adhanom, the Foreign Affairs Minister of the Federal Democratic Republic of Ethiopia, reminded delegates that the May 9th Agreement to resolve the crisis, committed all the parties to the principle of inclusivity and the involvement of key stakeholders from South Sudan in the peace process. "The region and the international community strongly believe that the only way to resolve the crisis in South Sudan is through genuine and inclusive political dialogue," said the Minister who was also the Chairman of the IGAD Council of Ministers.

He reiterated the commitment of the people and governments of the region and the development partners to assist the South

Sudanese to reach a solution that is sustainable and one that reflects their common vision. The symposium helped the stakeholders to understand their collective responsibility to restore peace in the country. It clarified the structural and principle issues to address. It also defined and identified the stakeholders and the importance of their participation in the process to attain sustainable peace in the country.

Besides the warring parties and other political forces, the following groups were identified: The women's block, civil society organizations, faith-based groups, and eminent personalities.

The talks then resumed with full participation of those groups. Despite the fact that the so-called non-partisan stakeholders were in one way or another affiliated with the warring parties, there was a general yearning for peace across the political and social spectra of South Sudan.

CHAPTER SEVEN

The Arusha Track

*"If a political party does not have its foundation in the deter-
mination to advance a cause that is right and that is moral,
then it is not a political party; it is merely a conspiracy to
seize power."*

Dwight D. Eisenhower

The Genesis of the Initiative

The Intra-SPLM dialogue that transpired as the Arusha Track was first initiated as SPLM Leadership Review and Self-Assessment Forum within the framework of the IGAD led peace process to run concurrently with the Addis Ababa Track. It was meant to provide a critical contribution to the broader political dialogue towards national reconciliation and healing.

Bringing in an advance team of SPLM Politburo members to meet and prepare for the SPLM Leadership Review and Self-Assessment Forum was proposed. The meeting was scheduled to take place on April 5, 2014, in Addis Ababa, under the auspices of H.E Hailemariam Desalegn, the Prime Minister of the Federal Democratic Republic of Ethiopia and the then Chairperson of the IGAD Assembly.

The proposed advance team was to develop the agenda, modalities and timeframe for the forum in order to address the underlying causes of the crisis in South Sudan. It was set to be facilitated by representatives of the Ethiopian People's Revolutionary Democratic Front (EPRDF) and the African National Congress (ANC). Both parties had background in transforming liberation movement into conventional political parties. A number of regional think-tanks and analysts believed that one of the biggest roadblocks to IGAD's peace process was the SPLM's internal crisis. They stressed that until these problems were addressed it would be difficult to get a comprehensive peace agreement.

The presumption was that the SPLM could serve as the unifying institution in South Sudan, overcoming the fissures that developed between President Kiir and Vice President Machar. The Arusha process, which operated parallel to that of IGAD had developed a set of principles that would allow for a new reunified SPLM government to be a vehicle for peace and reform. Location shopping ensued, and Tanzania was finally agreed upon to the most neutral and conducive ground for this process.

It was an obvious choice. For one thing, the country is a beacon of peace and democracy and the most stable overall in the region. A considerable factor was that it was a non-neighboring country without direct involvement in the conflict. Tanzania could provide honest mediation, which she did.

At the invitation of the Chairman of the ruling Chama Cha Mapinduzi (CCM), Ndugu Jakaya Merisho Kikwete, the Intra-SPLM-Party Dialogue was held in Arusha, Tanzania from October 12-18, 2014 to discuss and prepare the framework on the root causes of the SPLM internal crisis within the SPLM that had plunged the country into civil war. Said dialogue was facilitated by the CCM Secretary General, Ndugu Abdulrahman Kinana.

The preliminary meeting was attended by the representative delegations of the three SPLM factions: SPLM (IG), SPLM (FDs) and the SPLM (IO) and wasconcluded with the Arusha Communiqué on October 20, 2014 by all. The SPLM (IG) was represented by Cde. Akol Paul Kordit; the SPLM (IO) by Cde. Duer Tut Duer and the SPLM(FDs) by Cde. Pagan Amum Okiech.

The communiqué committed the tripartite factions to honest and frank dialogue and took collective responsibility for the crisis in the country. The results of the lengthy and cordial discussions are summarized as follows:

▌ The parties acknowledged a collective responsibility for the crisis in South Sudan that has taken a great toll on the lives and property of the people. The Parties also acknowledged that dialogue, rules, and procedures are the only means to resolve the internal differences and lack of consensus over important party issues among SPLM leaders.

▌ The parties underlined the important role of the SPLM as the party that led the fight for national liberation culminating in the freedom and independence of South Sudan. The parties also underscored the fact that a divided SPLM will automatically fragment the country along ethnic and regional fault lines. Therefore, the crisis must be urgently brought to an end by the SPLM collective leadership through genuine and honest dialogue that put the interest of the people and the nation above all.

▌ The parties committed themselves to an agenda and timeline for a follow-up meeting scheduled to take place within a fortnight (2 weeks) with the aim of expediting the process with utmost efficiency, determination, and commitment.

▌ The parties recognized that the Arusha process was essentially an Intra-SPLM Dialogue and is separate and distinct from the IGAD mediated peace talks.

The Arusha Accord
"Contradictions do not dissolve, they are resolved"

Professor Peter Adwok Nyaba

The Arusha Track was better mediated than the Addis Ababa Track simply because the mediating party, Chama Cha Mapinduzi (CCM), gave us an ample opportunity to frankly engage ourselves in discussions that took us back from the historical SPLM/A right through to the internal crisis at hand. This way we could provide our own solutions that would lead to permanent peace in South Sudan. The root causes of the crisis were discussed and identified.

The forum was recognized as an historic opportunity to take collective responsibility for all the ills that have befallen the SPLM/A since liberation. The root causes were identified as the lack of internal democracy perpetrated by a culture of silence, political militarism, and sectarianism.

Through factual presentation, mostly by the SPLM (IO) delegation, we reached a consensus that they were the fundamental problems complicating the democratization of the inter-SPLM political process and providing for a smooth succession.

The SPLM factions also recognized their collective failure regarding the governance and building strong state institutions that would enable nation-building. Unlike in Addis Ababa where it was the government versus the rebels, in Arusha it was the SPLM/A sorting itself out and discussing its problems openly. Here we became comrades.

Initially, the SPLM (IG) started out being very defensive. However, when we reached the depth of the debate pertaining to the historical and contemporary failures, many, with the exception of raw intellectuals like James Kok Ruei and Nunu Kambe saw sense in the need for reforms, reconciliation, and reunification.

In one case, James Kok furiously reacted to a presentation in which I said the SPLM is suffering from the pathology of the oppressed and what Professor Patrick Lumumba has called 'martyrs' syndrome'. Those two pathologies are common social disorders from which most African liberators suffer. The prior theorizes that the oppressed often imitate the oppressors to oppress themselves or their subjects long after the oppressor is vanquished. The later entails that the liberators always assume power with a sense of entitlement to rule its liberated subjects without accountability. The liberator does not expect to be accountable to anyone.

According to this martyr mentality, he is entitled to be the oppressor, and to loot and kill with impunity. That angered Kok, who took it as an insult to the party that liberated the people of South Sudan from bondage.

He and his cohorts fantasize over the erroneous theory that liberators have free reign over the liberated. This pathological mentality tends to recognize the SPLM/A as a distinct organization of heroes. Dr. Adwok reacted to Kok's outburst in a taunting manner by questioning his understanding of the English language when presenting those absurd theories. That angered Kok even more and he started banging the table. Some of us laughed it off, but it was a serious verbal confrontation that almost turned physical.

Another thing that annoyed the SPLM (IG) was the way we laughed to tears at Daniel Awet Akot's difficulty pronouncing Chama Cha Mapinduzi as "Chama-Chama-Chama". The whole reading of his keynote speech sounded like Thok e Jieng in English. As a side note, making a jest of a person's deficiencies in such a way was nothing we should be proud of. Everyone was on edge and these things happen.

I must also confess that we initially brought the Addis Ababa negativity to Arusha and we were equally aggressive. That made the first interactions stormy. However, the chairperson of the meeting intervened and we settled down to harmonize the discussions. Thusly, the meeting continued and went on smoothly.

After intense, lengthy negotiations, the tripartite factions of the SPLM finally reached the Arusha Accord on January 22, 2014, with the aim to reunify the SPLM.

The parties agreed on many contentious points including political, organizational and leadership issues. There were several objectives. The primary being to reunify all the disparate groups of the SPLM immediately and to undertake reforms in the party leading to reforms in the country.

The reunification agreement was signed by the parties and fueled optimism for peace locally and internationally. While the document did not necessarily address the immediate leadership contradictions within the party with detailed intervention strategies, it touched on the fundamental facets of reforms. The lack of which have fanned the fires of the crisis.

The "Agreement on the Reunification of the SPLM" (commonly referenced as a blueprint), was signed under the auspices of Tanzania's governing party. It attempted to reunify the SPLM through a conflict resolution mechanism.

A particularly appealing feature of the Agreement is that it commits the warring parties to accept having failed the people of South Sudan. Although the emphasis on AU Commission of Inquiry Reports (ACR) was dropped from the final version of the draft due to the concern of SPLM-IG re the consequences of the report of the AU Commission of Inquiry on the Conflict in South Sudan, we managed to agree on a comprehensive Transitional Justice Process to prosecute those who have committed atrocities and war crimes.

Ultimately, it was agreed upon that any party member convicted in a court of law would be barred from holding public office on the SPLM ticket. The framework focuses on 44 reforms broadly classified as political, organizational, and leadership. By signing the

Agreement, the SPLM faction committed themselves to strictly adhering to the Cessation of Hostilities agreement accelerating the peace process and apologizes to the South Sudanese general public for failing their liberation aspirations and for assaulting them.

The Agreement commits the SPLM leadership to publicly apologize to the people of South Sudan and acknowledgment of their individual roles in the genesis of the current mayhem in the country. This was seen as a road toward healing and reconciliation.

The other noteworthy political commitments included investing in reconciliation and healing programs, combating political corruption, and embracing internal democracy, amongst others.

The agreement stresses combating militarism and sectarianism in national political life and freeing up space for creating an environment that promotes political pluralism. Re the organizational aspect, the agreement dealt with the party's need for restructuring to engender coherence, discipline, and to promote an independent, internal bureaucracy within party structures.

More specifically, the Agreement limits the authority of the party's chair, outlaws a "show of hands" voting model on contentious matters and institutionalizes the organization by vesting more power in the Political Bureau.

The Agreement also makes interesting pronouncements regarding the effect of separating the party from the SPLA and the country's defense force in such a manner that military commanders could not hold positions within the party.

The leaders' recognition of this anomaly was an about-face. If upheld in the agreement's implementation, this would go a long way towards healing. That clause was meant to professionalize the security sector for effective national security sector reform. On the leadership side of things, the SPLM committed to limiting the chairpersons' term, widened political competition space, adopted general elections for all positions, instituted committees to manage a range of internal bureaucracies, commissioned the Tripartite Committee to direct the execution of the Agreement, and authorized Chama Cha Mapinduzi as a principal guarantor of the Agreement. It closed with a matrix that details the implementation mechanism for each area agreed upon.

Dissecting the Arusha Accord

The agreement was concluded at the time when all the previous talks in Addis Ababa floundered. Hence, it does no justice to analyze it without considering the internal and external circumstances that pushed the parties to move out of their defensive trenches and meet halfway.

One of those factors was the international pressure mounting on the antagonists. Those countries and bodies were frustrated by the lack of progress made in the IGAD talks, the continuous violation of the CoH and the growing humanitarian crisis.

The Intra-SPLM Dialogue took place at the backdrop of the resolution of the 28th Summit of IGAD Heads of States and Governments in Addis Ababa. The parties were warned to either stop the war or risk punitive sanctions and direct intervention by the region to protect civilians and impose peace and stability.

Further afield, there were consultative discussions at the UN Security Council level to impose sanctions on the Government of South Sudan and the SPLM (IO) for obstruction of the peace process and causing suffering in the populace. As well, neighboring countries such as Uganda and Kenya were under pressure from their citizens to end the conflict. Juba was truly suffering under pariah status.

Among the many timely internal factors was that the CCM provided a conducive environment for the SPLM factions where they had a rare opportunity to engage themselves in intense and frank debate. They had never had such an opportunity since the Rumbek meeting of 2004. There, an imminent crisis was resolved through open and frank dialogue. Those who know the SPLM/A from the inside can attest to the fact that the Arusha debate brought the best out of a movement that rarely took the chance to look inward.

Through those free debates, the SPLM rediscovered itself as a liberation movement theoretically founded on democratic principle and institutions it never practiced preaching since its inception. The SPLM factions also came to realize that their violent divisions wreaked havoc on the social fabric of South Sudan. The need for internal unity was critical for peace.

The aim was to bring about a reunited party. The agreement made considerable strides towards that as well as reconciliation and peace. Its shortcoming was the raging war. Thus, Article 19 of the Accord stipulated that the reunification of the SPLM was conditional on the conclusion of a peace agreement in Addis Ababa.

Obviously, a party that is fighting itself cannot realize organic unity right away. However, Article 9 of the Arusha agreement resolved critical issues regarding power sharing that were difficult for the seniority in the SPLM hierarchy. This meant that with the reinstatement of the dismissed leaders, other things would fall into place. That was why we changed our negotiating position for the Executive Prime Minister. Unfortunately, the agreement has also proved that the issue of leadership continues to be the greatest challenge facing all efforts for the reunification of the SPLM. Article 40 of the agreement stipulated that: "The structure of the leadership of the reunified SPLM will have to be worked out by the CCM and the three principals."

Public Reaction to the Arusha Accord

The agreement took many observers by surprise and was received with mixed reactions. Skeptics maintained that a party whose division caused so much damage to the social fabric of South Sudan couldn't come together just like that.

Represented in these pessimistic views were those who agreed with Deng Athuai that neither a split nor reunification of the decayed SPLM Party could bring any hope to the people of South Sudan as they loot when they unite and kill when they split. I shared that view to some extent but thought the SPLM should be given the benefit of the doubt as a mechanism to attempt to unite the nation once again.

The optimists, on the other hand, mainly SPLM members, thought that the Arusha Agreement has done the magic to unite the party and the country. Most applauded in the agreement was the SPLM leaders' acceptance to take responsibility for the party's loss of vision, lack of internal democracy and not living up to the people's post-independence expectations of liberation rewards. Above all they lauded the agreement to work hard to ensure that measures of accountability and justice were established and enforced.

Regarding the accountability, it positively astonished many that the agreement called for exclusion from party offices, and subsequently from the executive, anyone who is found by a competent court to have had involvement in, or was responsible for, atrocities or crimes against humanity. As mentioned previously, it committed the SPLM leadership to make a public apology for what happened since December 15, 2013, and to ensure the prosecution of those involved in war crimes and atrocities.

Some analysts observed that the commitment of the parties that signed the agreement to accountability on war crimes was half-hearted. There is also the obvious fact that the SPLM (IG) had rejected Transitional Justice in Addis Ababa. Most interestingly, Article 17 of the Arusha Accord stipulated that in order to ensure that executive powers in Government are not negatively used to influence or determine Party matters, all decisions affecting the Party shall be taken only through Puny structures.

This was a very important provision as that was what Salva Kiir did in December 2013. He used state executive powers to persecute his political opponents during the run-up to the national convention.

In any case, Kiir was not happy at the time of signing the Arusha Agreement. The war had intensified that week resulting in the defeat of his forces at Doleb Hill by the SPLM (IO). As such, he signed while in a fighting mood. His speech was loaded with talk of war and violence.

Difficulties with the implementation of the Arusha Track would not take long to surface. From the tone of the press conference at Juba International Airport upon his arrival, it quickly became evident that President Kiir dishonored the principles agreed to in the process. In fact, Kiir's body language during the signing ceremony in Arusha spoke volumes of his intention to violate it. In any case, there is no denying that the accord was a giant step toward the reunification of the SPLM factions and expediting the peace process as the same three groups that agreed in Arusha were the very political stakeholders negotiating in Addis Ababa.

However, reading things by Kiir's mental and physical attitude while signing the agreement, many could tell that it would be faced with real challenges. As for the SPLM (IO), I knew the harsh reality on the ground was that the reunification of the SPLM was not very popular among our political and military leaders in Pagak. In fact, the agreement was openly opposed by our field commanders fighting for the regime change as was resolved in the last Pagak Conference.

Some key senior IO generals such as General Stephen Parr Kuol made public remarks casting doubt regarding their commitment to it. Kiir himself did not feel that the agreement would result in a reunification of the SPLM.

He stated: "I would like to say we would continue to work with CCM to learn from their experiences. However, I don't think that we are yet to be united. I will believe it only when we sit in one place".

His speeches around that time were full of war talk, not peace.

As with previous agreements, the President quickly reneged from the principles agreed upon in Arusha. Kiir's body language at the podium demonstrated his ill intentions to violate it, and he did.

Pagan Amum, after returning to Juba to implement the agreement had to flee in fear for his own life once again after being frustrated by Kiir's SPLM (IG). He had this to say: "I returned to Juba in July 2015 to implement the Arusha Accord but upon meeting with Kiir, I found that he had turned into a tribal dictator. He was willing neither to redress the grave mistakes he had committed and involved us in, nor to reach a peace accord or to achieve national reconciliation to mend the social fabric and restore peace among the South Sudanese people."

Members of Tanzania's ruling party, Chama Cha Mapinduzi, worked with representatives from the Crisis Management Initiative, a Finnish conflict resolution organization founded by Martti Ahtisaari.

The Diplomacy of Arusha Track was characterized by forum shopping and competition among African states, including South Africa, which actively backed the Arusha process.

See Article 19 of the Arusha Accord stipulating that the reunification of the SPLM is conditional upon completion of the Addis Ababa Process and resolution of the conflict.

CHAPTER EIGHT

The Mounting International Pressure on the Parties

For over 18 months, the mediation team composed of the special envoys of regional IGAD struggled to secure a deal amidst deep regional divisions and the parties' truculence. All the talks floundered by March 2015 amidst the humanitarian and security crisis on the ground in South Sudan.

The regional leaders under the guidance of Prime Minister Desalegn Haile Mariam (Ethiopia) started using threatening language while making it very clear that they were running out of patience with the two major warring parties. They then formally invited the principals of said parties to Addis Ababa to commit themselves to a peaceful settlement of the conflict. When they arrived a series of proxy negotiations ensued culminating in a May 9, 2014 Agreement to resolve the crisis through peaceful means. This communiqué of the IGAD Assembly Heads of State and Government signed on June 10, 2014.

Upon arrival in Juba, Salva Kiir disclosed that he and Riek Machar initialed the DOPS peace deal in Addis-Ababa to avoid threats of arrest by the Ethiopian Prime Minister.

The peace process fully collapsed by March 2015. Prime Minister Haile Mariam wrote a strongly worded letter to the people of South Sudan saying he regretted the careless and selfish attitude of their leaders. General Lazarus Sumbeiywo, the IGAD Special envoy representing Kenya expressed extreme emotion and said: "South Sudan has gone to the dogs and I want to walk naked with anger against the South Sudanese leaders who tend to be scavenging on the death of their own people."

To overcome these challenges, IGAD announced a revised, expanded mediation "IGAD-PLUS". It would include the African Union, the UN, China, the USA, the UK, the European Union, Norway and the IGAD Partners Forum (IPF). The initiative was designed to present a united international front behind IGAD to the warring sides. Unfortunately, it did not gain the necessary backing from the wider international community. This disillusioned both IGAD and the South Sudanese leaders on both sides of the conflict.

Rather than distancing itself from IGAD, the international community needed to support a realistic, regionally centered strategy to end the war, underpinned by coordinated threats. It was that expanded mediation that produced an agreement in August 2015, the Agreement for the Resolution of the Conflict in the Republic of South Sudan (ARCSS) (IGAD, 2015).

There were circumstances that pushed the parties to rethink their calculations. At that point in time, the region and international community were frustrated by the lack of progress made in the IGAD mediated peace talks and the continuous violation of the Cessation of Hostilities Agreement. All this was occurring while a sizeable portion of the population of South Sudan was under the threat of war-induced hunger.

This was the backdrop of the Resolution of the 28th Summit of IGAD Heads of State and Government held in Addis Ababa in November. It warned the parties either to stop the war or risk punitive sanctions and direct intervention by the region in South Sudan to protect civilians and to impose peace and stability. This was a landmark decision as those countries had been hesitant until then to impose sanctions. Some countries in the West have taken the lead on that, albeit targeting the small fry.

Creating a new AU body comprising of the heads of states representing all five regions of the continent to assist the IGAD mediation followed their summit decision. That was followed by the submission of the report of the AU Commission of Inquiry on the Conflict in South Sudan to the AU Commission. Further afield, there were consultative discussions at the UN Security Council level to impose sanctions on the government of South Sudan and rebels who would obstruct peace and cause suffering to the population.

What was being debated was not just the idea but the nature of the sanctions to be imposed. Indeed, the European Union went ahead and imposed an arms embargo on South Sudan. Other countries including Uganda were under pressure from their public to follow suit. Subsequently, Museveni abandoned his own proposal that he had been pushing through to support Kiir's position. Under all that intense diplomatic pressure, Salva Kiir was being equated with the rebel leader, Dr. Machar as pariahs.

Having lost the debate at the table, the international community agreed with the opposition and other stakeholders that there was a need for reforms and democratic change in South Sudan. President Salva Kiir then became the unhappiest man of the year. He perceived the whole thing as a conspiracy for regime change. True, it is difficult to delink change and reforms from regime change. However, the change we meant then was a constructive one through agreed transitional arrangements.

Upon the receipt of the first draft of the Compromise Agreement, Kiir wrote a desperately worded circular to most of the head of states and governments expressing the sentiment of his government against it. In response, Kiir was then diplomatically pressured into deep and meaningful discussions by the regional leaders and TRIOKA regarding acceptance of the peace process.

Eventually, he was persuaded to travel to Addis Ababa to sign. However, upon arrival, he changed his mind and refused. He finally signed it ten days later in Juba. Immediately following, he said he had some reservations against it and that it was neither a Koran nor a Bible. He also made statements reflecting his unwillingness to unify the SPLM pursuant to the Arusha Accords and return to SPLM's vision.

CHAPTER NINE

The Key Provisions of ARCSS

Conventional wisdom on conflict resolution contends that no party can get all it hopes for in any negotiated settlement. Hence, those of us who negotiated ARCSS on the opposition side, as well as the mediation and technical experts who drafted the compromise agreement, reached a consensus that it offered a comprehensive, balanced, political settlement that did indeed compromise to end the crisis in South Sudan. It constituted the transitional political and security arrangements required to bring about lasting peace.

The timeframe for its implementation was 33 months. The agreement is divided into 6 thematic areas negotiated over 14 months during 21 rounds of intensive talks. Those areas are Transitional Governance, Permanent Ceasefire, Transitional Security Arrangements, Humanitarian Assistance, Resources, Economic and Financial Management, Transitional Justice, Accountability, Reconciliation and Healing, and the Parameters for the Permanent Constitutional Making Process. The parties include the GRSS, SPLM (IO), SPLM (FDs) and the other political parties. Below is a summary of some of the provisions that make up ARCSS.

Chapter I – Governance and Power Sharing

Chapter I of ARCSS establishes Transitional Governance in the form of the Transitional Government of National Unity (TGoNU) with the following power-sharing arrangements:

It provides for the GRSS to maintain a majority in the legislature, the position of the Vice President and 53 percent of the ministerial portfolios.

The SPLM (IO) are to have the second largest share of power and seats in the Transitional National Assembly, the First President and 33 percent of the ministerial portfolios. As stipulated in Article (6.1)

The SPLM (FDs) receive 7% and the other political parties receive 7%.

ARCSS also provided for the expansion of the Transitional Legislature for the duration of the transitional period comprising of 400 members. This would include the existing 332 plus an additional 68 representatives appointed according via the following criteria: SPLM/A (IO): 50; SPLM (FDs): 1; Other Political Parties: 17. The mandate of the TGONU is to accomplish the following:

- Implement this Agreement to restore peace, security, and stability in the country.
- Expedite relief, protection, voluntary and dignified repatriation, rehabilitation and resettlement of IDPs and returnees.
- Facilitate and oversee a process of national reconciliation and healing through an independent mechanism in accordance with this Agreement including budgetary provisions for compensation and reparations.
- Oversee and ensure the Permanent Constitution-Making process is successfully carried out.
- Work closely with the IGAD-PLUS Member States and Organizations, other partners and friends of South Sudan, to consolidate peace and stability in the country.
- Reform of public financial management.
- Ensure prudent, transparent and accountable management of national wealth and resources to build the nation and promote the welfare of the people

▌ Rebuild the destroyed physical infrastructure in conflict-affected areas and give special attention to prioritizing the rebuilding of livelihoods of those affected by the conflict.

▌ Establish a competent and impartial National Elections Commission (NEC) to conduct free and fair elections before the end of the Transitional Period and to ensure that the outcome is broadly reflective of the will of the electorate.

▌ Make all efforts to conduct a National Population and Housing Census before the end of the Transitional Period, while taking into account Article 16.9 of this Agreement.

▌ Devolve power and resources to State and County level.

Chapter II -Transitional Security Arrangement and Permanent Ceasefire

Pursuant to Chapter II Article (1.8, 1.8.8, 1.5) of the Agreement on the Conflict Resolution in South Sudan (CRISS), the core to the implementation of the Transitional Security Arrangement is the demilitarization of the major centers including Juba, Bor, Bentiu and Malakal.

Read together with Article 5 (5.2, 5 & 1.1.3) and the minutes of Addis Ababa Security Workshop dated September 17-27, 2015, these key provisions have not only granted management of public security to the Joint Integrated Police but also authorized a total of 3,000 police personnel in each of the said locations. ARCSS establishes transitional security armament institutions and a mechanism of implementations.

There will be a Joint Military Ceasefire Commission (JMCC) staffed with four Deputy Chiefs of General Staff. Two from the GRSS forces and two from the SPLM/A (IO) forces. It shall be responsible for oversight and coordination of forces in cantonment for as long as they are required to be bivouacked there. It shall report to the Commanders in Chief of the GRSS Forces and SPLM/A (IO) forces.

The Area Joint Military Ceasefire Committee (AJMCC) and The Joint Military Ceasefire Team (JMCT), are to be located at the State and Unit levels respectively in Juba, Jonglei, Unity, and Upper Nile States. The Joint Military Ceasefire Team (JMCT), shall be reporting to Area Joint Military Ceasefire Committee (AJMCC) who shall also be reporting to JMCC.

The Ceasefire and Transitional Security Arrangements Monitoring Mechanism (CTSAMM) responsible for reporting on the progress of the implementation of the Permanent Ceasefire and Transitional Security Arrangements (PCTSA) and monitoring compliance are to report directly to the Joint Monitoring and Evaluation Commission (JMEC) on the progress of the implementation of the PCTSA.

Chapter III: Humanitarian Assistance and Reconstruction

The parties and the stakeholders agreed that during the Pre-Transitional and Tranistional Periods the GRSS and the Opposition shall create an enabling political, administrative, operational and legal environment for the delivery of humanitarian assistance and protection. In addition to the Permanent Ceasefire obligations described in Chapter II, the GRSS, the South Sudan commiteed themselves to ensuring the following:

- Secure access to civilian populations in need of emergency humanitarian assistance and protection;
- The right of refugees and Internally Displaced Persons (IDPs) to return in safety and dignity and to be afforded physical, legal and psychological protection;

▌ The rights of returnees shall be respected in accordance with the Bill of Rights as provided for in the Transitional Constitution (TCRSS). Given that, efforts shall be made to assist in the re-unification of family members who were separated during the conflict;

▌ The right of refugees and IDPs to citizenship and the establishment of mechanisms for registration and appropriate identification and/or documentation of affected populations including their children, spouses, property, land and other possessions which might have been lost during the . Exercise of the right of refugees and IDPs to return to their places of origin and/or live in areas of their choice in safety and dignity;

▌ Under the same chapter, it is stipulated that the TGoNU, in collaboration and support of international partners and friends of South Sudan, shall establish a Special Fund for Reconstruction (SRF) within the first (one) month of the Transition, to be administered by the Board of Special Reconstruction Fund (BSRF), comprising of membership drawn from the TGoNU and international partners of South Sudan. :

Chapter V: Transitional Justice, Accountability, Reconciliation and Healing.

To end the impunity for the crimes committed during the course of this conflict, ARCSS commits the African Union, the United Nations and the Transitional Government of National Unity to jointly establish an independent hybrid judicial body, to be known as the Hybrid Court for South Sudan (HCSS) with jurisdiction over war crimes, crimes against humanity and other serious crimes committed under international law since 2005.

This meant that the TGoNU committed to fully cooperate and seek the assistance of the African Union, the United Nations and the African Commission on Human and People's Rights to design, implement and facilitate the work of the agreed transitional justice mechanisms provided for in the Agreement. In accordance with this provision, the judges of the HCSS will be selected and appointed by the United Nations Secretary-General and the AU Chairperson. The Transitional Justice protocol also provides for the following transitional justice institutions:

The Commission for Truth, Reconciliation, and Healing (CTRH)

This shall be established by legislation, which shall be promulgated not later than six (6) months after the formation of the TGoNU and commence its activities not later than a month thereafter. The CTRH is mandated to independently promote the common objective of facilitating truth, reconciliation and healing, compensation and reparation in South Sudan.

The ultimate goal is to address the legacy of the conflicts, promote peace, national reconciliation and healing.

Chapter IV - Key institutional reforms

ARCSS commits the TGoNU to institutional and legal reforms of key public institutions in terms of leadership composition, independence, power, function, and operations. The Ministry of Petroleum, The National Petroleum and Gas Cooperation, The Bank of South Sudan, The Anti-Corruption Commission and The National Audit Chamber will be reformed to ensure sound management of the economy.

ARCSS targets the Petroleum Sector for thorough reforms.

This is important for micro-economic stability. Pursuant to The Transitional Institution and Mechanism, the following pre-existing Commissions and Institutions shall be reconstituted at the national level, as provided for in the Agreement. Within the first month of the TGoNU, the Executive shall supervise and facilitate the reforms and reconstitutions of the following Commissions and Institutions paying particular attention to the mandates and appointments, to ensure their independence and accountability:

- Anti-Corruption Commission (ACC)
- Public Grievances Chamber (PGC)
- Fiscal, Financial Allocation and Monitoring Commission (FFAMC)
- National Audit Chamber (NAC)
- Relief and Rehabilitation Commission (RRC)
- Peace Commission (PC)
- National Bureau of Statistics (NBS)
- Human Rights Commission (HRC)
- Judicial Service Commission (JSC)
- Civil Service Commission (CSC)
- Land Commission (LC)
- Electric Corporation (EC)
- Refugees Commission (RC)
- National Corporation for Radio and Television (NCRT)
- National Petroleum and Gas Corporation (NPGC)
- Bureau of Standards (BS)

Review of National Legislative Acts

To ensure that the institutional reform is implemented, ARCSS commits the TGoNU to the reviews and amendment of following legislative acts:

- Investment Promotion Act - 2009
- Banking Act - 2010
- Telecommunications Act - 2010
- The Transport Act – 2008
- The National Audit Chambers Act.
- Anti-Corruption Commission Act
- Public Finance Management and Accountability Act
- Petroleum Act
- The Mining Act

Chapter VII - Parameters for the creation of a permanent Constitution.

One of the major mandates of the TGoNU is to oversee the permanent constitutional making process based on democracy and the rules of law. The parameters of this dictate that the process must be broad-based and ethnically inclusive to reflect the national diversity of South Sudan. It must be a people-driven process with a transparent mechanism for public consultation, constitutional conferences, and constituent assemblies. The process must be completed not later than 12 months before the end of the transitional period to guide the election which should be held within 6 days thereafter.

Chapter VIII - Supremacy of ARCSS

This chapter deals with the supremacy of the agreement over all existing national legislation. This means that in the event the provisions of the TCoSS and the law conflict, the terms of ARCSS shall prevail. In compliance with the procedure outlined in Chapter I,

Article 4 the agreement, ARCSS must be fully incorporated within the Transitional Constitution for it to obtain legal force. Once incorporated it will be the supreme law of the land pursuant to Chapter VII.

ARCSS can be amended with a majority of at least two-thirds of the members of the Council of Ministers, and, at least two-thirds of the voting members of the Joint Monitoring and Evaluation Commission (JMEC). This is to be followed by ratification by the Transitional National Assembly, all according to the constitutional amendment procedure set out in the TCoSS, 2011.

In theory, ARCSS has everything in place to fix South Sudan and steer it towards the path of permanent peace and prosperity. It has laid out major institutional reforms including national security and financial management, accountability, reconciliation and healing, and federal sectors. This includes installing a democratic system of governance and devolution of power during the interim period. ARCSS also provides for the establishment of a Compensation and Reparation Authority for the victims of the conflict, provision of relief assistance protection, voluntary and dignified repatriation, rehabilitation and resettlement of IDPs and returnees.

Ultimately, it gives the people of South Sudan an opportunity to write their own permanent constitution and elect their own leaders at the end of the transitional period.

The structural content of the ARCSS included chapters on: (1) a transitional government, (2) a permanent cease-fire and transitional security arrangements, (3) humanitarian assistance and 23, reconstruction, (4) economic and financial management, (5) transitional justice, (6) a permanent constitution, and (7) joint monitoring and evaluation, as well as eight corresponding implementation appendices. "Agreement on the Resolution of the Conflict in the Republic of South Sudan," Addis Ababa, Ethiopia, 17 August 2015.

CHAPTER TEN

Signing Under Duress

The Inconclusive Signing Ceremony in Addis Ababa

As the internationally and regionally set deadline of August 17 approached, President Museveni broke silence regarding his cynical views on the IGAD mediation by inviting his Kenyan and Ethiopian counterparts to Uganda for yet another summit on August 10. This had the effect of smearing the process and angering the mediators, the South Sudanese opposition and the other stakeholders.

In the attempt to impose his will on the region and the mediations, Museveni proposed substantial changes to the draft agreement already under review by the parties. These included alterations to the proposed power-sharing formulas and, more consequentially, to its prescribed security arrangements. This included softening or deferring of provisions for the integration of forces, the demilitarization of Juba, and the introduction of a third-party force to provide security for transitional institutions in the capital city. Many of these issues were deferred to two deeply flawed workshops on security. They were nominally "technical" exercises that occurred after the accord was finalized and wider attention had subsided.

On the deadline date, after several weeks of focused international attention, Dr. Riek Machar, together with a representative of the SPLM (FDs), signed the accord on behalf of the opposition. President Kenyatta was quite agitated and confronted President Kiir. As could be easily seen in a photo taken at the event, the body language of the two of them gave a clear indication of their thoughts.

Kenyatta was pressuring Kiir to sign but the South Sudanese president was unready to commit. As a result, the Ethiopian and Kenyan leaders decided to afford him two additional weeks to return to Juba and secure the needed support from his hardliners to allow him to sign the deal.

In the ensuing days, the United States introduced a draft resolution in the UN Security Council threatening an arms embargo and targeted sanctions against South Sudan if the government failed to finalize the deal. Nine days later at a ceremony in Juba, Kiir, while citing a series of 'reservations', signed the agreement in the presence of the IGAD leaders. This ended the second phase of the process.

Despite notable flaws, including eleventh-hour changes to the security protocol, the 'Agreement on the Resolution of the Conflict' outlined a plan to end the fighting, frame a post-conflict transition and begin the tasks of reconciliation and reform. As such, it reflected the objectives that guided the mediators during Phase II of the peace process.

Nonetheless, the agreement collapsed in July 2016.

On June 12, 2015, IGAD (PLUS) unveiled a proposed draft agreement between president Salva Kiir's government and the SPLM (IO). The draft copy was presented as: "Key provisions and justification for the agreement on the resolution of the conflict in the Republic of South Sudan." It also included power-sharing for former detainees (FDs) and other political parties (PPs).

The draft agreement proposed to maintain Kiir as head of state while the opposition leader, Machar, would become the First Vice President. The incumbent James Wani Igga would also continue as a Vice President. The parties would negotiate executive powers or roles between the three top executive branches.

Kiir objected to the draft and in a televised address to the nation said was a violation of the sovereignty of the Republic of South

Sudan and that he would never sign it. However, amidst rising international pressure and threats of more sanctions, Kiir reversed his decision and traveled to Addis Ababa. Again, he evaded signing by demanding a 15-day extension.

After lengthy consultations with the SPLM (IO) delegation plus other leaders present in Ethiopia, Dr. Machar signed the document along with the FDs, women's blocks and other stakeholders as Kiir watched in confusion and despair. The negotiations were then left with half a peace agreement. Mama Rebecca Nyandeang fumed and cried out in contempt of the president. She called him a selfish leader who does not care about the death and suffering of his people.

The Gloomy Signing Ceremony in Juba

Peace agreements are usually signed with smiles, hopes or even with euphoric ululations by women in South Sudanese culture. Sadly, the atmosphere was rather different during the ceremony in Juba. President Kiir made it painstakingly clear how little faith he had in it.

Kiir again announced that he had serious reservations. With a straight face, he handed a twelve-page document out to the assembled dignitaries. It was intended to be an addendum to the peace deal. However, the US and others quickly made it clear they would not accept any changes to the signed text.

Contained in this 'addendum' was concern regarding demilitarization of the major centers (including Juba) as stipulated in Chapter II Article (1.8,1.8.8,1.5) of the Agreement and the power-sharing matrix that compelled him to consult the first vice-president, Dr. Riek Machar on key policy issues.

In a very ranting and undiplomatic tone, Kiir stated that the negotiations were handled "carelessly" by regional and world leaders. He went on to threaten that: "A poor agreement like this ARCSS could backfire on the region at any time". He also hurled in "intimidating messages" without specifying the source and said these constituted "a designed roadmap for regime change".

The message was clear. Kiir was signing under duress. Without a negotiated political settlement, many were wondering how long the deal would hold. Politically speaking, the President and his camp had more to lose than the SPLM (IO). Under this deal, Salva's political allies in the government would go from controlling the entire government to merely a majority. They would not even have that in Unity, Upper Nile, and Jonglei states. There, the government would have only 46% of the seats in the state legislature.

The opposition would also name the governors of oil-rich Unity and Upper Nile. This meant Kiir was on his own to manage the anger of his people who would lose their jobs and of those who felt ARCSS should not have been signed in the first place.

One of them was Michael Makuei Lueth, the information minister. He is a hardliner who reportedly walked of the signing ceremony in disgust. The chief of staff of the national army, Paul Malong, did attend the ceremony and was the subject of intense scrutiny. He, other generals, and the JCE elders were openly against ARCSS.

Salva's 15-day grace period of consultations and even his attempt to annex reservations to the agreement could be construed as an attempt to overcome the misgivings of the powerful interest groups within his camp who opposed it.

The regional leaders ignored that problem and instead congratulated the leaders of the Republic of South Sudan on reaching a political settlement. In comments echoed by Ugandan President Yoweri Museveni and Ethiopian Prime Minister Hailemariam Desalegn, Kenyan President Uhuru Kenyatta said it was a "happy day for us in the region" that the deal had been signed, and that South Sudan's leaders now need to focus on the future.

In response, the international community reacted accordingly. The UN Secretary General, Ban Ki-moon, welcomed the signing of the peace deal but his spokesman reading his statement noted that it must yet be implemented. "Now is the time to ensure that this agreement translates into an end to the violence, hardship and horrific human rights violations witnessed throughout this conflict."

Ms. Susan Rice, President Barack Obama's national security adviser, said the United States welcomed the deal as a "first step" towards ending the conflict, but that it would take "hard work" to implement the agreement. "However, we do not recognize any reservations or addendums to that agreement. We will work with our international partners to sideline those who stand in the way of peace, drawing upon the full range of our multilateral and bilateral tools."

US State Department spokesman John Kirby went a step further, saying that if Kiir acted on his reservations and reneged on the deal, the US would support further UN sanctions. He did not give specifics. The US had proposed a UN arms embargo and more sanctions from September 6th onward unless the pact was signed by the new deadline.

Those of us who participated in the negotiation of ARCSS made presentations and informed all concerned that it created a rare opportunity to reform the existing political and institutional estab-lishment in South Sudan. We managed to convince the mediation team that for South Sudan to become a viable and prosperous nation, the issues of bad governance, corruption and the militariza-tion of political spheres must be addressed. In sum, ARCSS was our brainchild. We crafted it to fix South Sudan. It is an agreement that created a judicial process in the form of a 'hybrid' court for South Sudan. This provision was framed to end the impunity with which both military and political leaders have acted. Our fear was based on the lukewarm attitude of the government toward this good agreement. With the permanent ceasefire not holding, we could see the whole shaky edifice tumbling down over disagreements within the transitional government. After all, the SPLM/A had a track-record of resorting to political violence and chaos rather than reaching any sort of amicable solution to a conflict. Our fears became reality when all hell broke loose on July 8, 2016.

CHAPTER ELEVEN

Making Sense
of Kiir's Reservations

The 16 reservations presented by President Kiir to be annexed to the agreement were largely swept aside by the guarantors and the international community. They rejected them outright while forgetting the danger they posed. The guarantors forgot the ugly truth that without wielding their big sticks over the parties to implement the agreement as promised, Kiir could disown it at will and that is exactly what he did. Even in the ARCSS preamble, the parties to the agreement were expected to acknowledge "the need to promote inclusivity and popular ownership of this Agreement", to ensure effective implementation. The simple and logical question was: How could the SPLM (IO) and other stakeholders implement the agreement without the collective ownership of the agreement with the SPLM (IG)? That was a very fundamental question left unasked and unanswered by none other than the guarantors of the agreement in the region and beyond. The other mind-numbing question is how could an agreement signed under duress be implemented without duress?

One of Kiir's most serious reservations was regarding the scope of the permanent ceasefire and transitional security arrangements. It was imposed on him after his delegation rejected the clauses during the negotiation. Article 5.5 of ARCSS provides for the redeployment of military forces within Juba. All others were to be outside of a 25 km radius.

That was another contentious issue we failed to agree upon. Kiir and his cronies interpreted that as disarmament of their police state, which is a "matter of sovereignty". In one of his typical blusters, President Kiir stated that the army "protected the capital during a failed coup". This was groundless given that the fact that ARCSS Article 5 (5.1) includes exceptions allowing the presidential guard's forces to protect military barracks, bases, and warehouses. These forces also included the Joint Integrated Police. Together, they were enough to defend the sovereignty of South Sudan.

Kiir's statements were contrary to the spirit of peace and reconciliation. He said all that in denial of the revelations contained in the Final Report of the AU Commission of Inquiry on South Sudan. It stated that there was not any available evidence to suggest an attempted coup had occurred in South Sudan. Those who understand Kiir could discern that his constant reference to the "failed coup" was a signal that mistrust and suspicion continued to characterize his working relationship with Dr. Machar and the other opposition parties in the TGoNU.

He also objected to the status of the monitoring and verification mechanism (MVM), which is responsible for reporting progress reimplementation of the permanent ceasefire and transitional security arrangements (PCTSA) to the ceasefire and the transitional security arrangement monitoring mechanism (CTSAMM).

In his document of reservations, Kiir objected to the MVM role, arguing that its current performance was unsatisfactory as its reports were based on unofficial information. He further suggested that the MVM transition to CTSAMM should only be based on government approval.

Too much reliance on unofficial information and statistics regarding reporting on security matters can be detrimental to peace efforts. Such information is often exaggerated and manipulated in pursuit of narrow partisan interests and external conspiracies against the state.

Pursuant to Chapter VII (2.7) of ARCSS, an independent

and representative Joint Monitoring and Evaluation Commission (JMEC) would oversee the work of CTSAMM. Hence, progressive and constructive discussions should be focused on strengthening the JMEC's capacity to execute its oversight role, instead of injecting government interference into the transition of MVM.

Kiir also had reservations about the roles and functions of the JMEC. According to Chapter VII (3) of ARCSS, it is responsible for "monitoring and overseeing the implementation of the Agreement, the mandate and tasks of the TGoNU, including the adherence of the parties to the agreed timelines and implementation schedule." He objected to the term: "oversight function of JMEC in the imple-mentation process." According to him, this would make the JMEC: "The governing authority of the Republic of South Sudan," leaving the government and national legislature uninvolved.

Furthermore, the President maintained that the provisions under Chapter VII (5) of ARCSS, mandates the JMEC to report regularly in writing to the TGoNU Council of Ministers and the Transitional National Assembly as well as IGAD, the AU Commission, the AU Peace and Security Council (PSC) and the UN Security Council (UNSC) on the status of implementation of the Agreement makes the JMEC "the actual ruling entity in South Sudan."

This is also nonsensical as all political parties in South Sudan were to be represented in the JMEC and would be part of the deliberations. Moreover, Chapter VII (9) clearly provides that the JMEC quorum "be 18, of which at least 10 of the members shall be from South Sudan and the other 8 from regional and international groups." This makes the JMEC agenda, proceedings and outcomes national and/or regional in outlook, thus dispelling sovereignty threats and fears.

Legally speaking, Kiir was demanding the impossible in his quest to assign his government the role to oversee the functions of the JMEC. This was an institution that the mediators attempted to make independent and impartial, with minimum interference from the implementers of ARCSS. Doing it his way would mean the government monitoring and evaluating itself. This would also make the JMEC vulnerable to governmental manipulation. The amendment procedure for ARCSS, as stipulated under Chapter VIII (Article 4), provides that the agreement can only be amended with at least a two-thirds majority of the Council of Ministers and at least a two-thirds majority of votes in the JMEC.

Kiir strongly objected to this. He considered this arrangement as "effectively neo-colonialism" and confirmed "the supremacy of the JMEC over the TGoNU and the national legislature." His objections were motivated by his intent to unilaterally amend ARCSS and to implement his reservations. That is what he did in the end.

From within the agreement, this was a technical impossibility given the fact that the SPLM/A (IG) just had only two out of the 18 members who make up the JMEC quorum. IG has 16 ministers out of the total of 30 ministers prescribed by Chapter 1 (Article 10) of ARCSS to make up the Council of Ministers. The amendment procedure involves two well-balanced institutions in terms of composition and structure in the form of the Council of Ministers and the JMEC. This is the essence as the agreement stipulates a checks and balances mechanism against politically motivated unilateral amendments. If proposed amendments are well thought out and progressive, there is no doubt that the procedures put in place would shepherd them through the system.

That had been rejected by his delegation during the peace talks in Addis Ababa. Kiir also registered his reservations on The Compensation and Reparation Authority (CRA) provided under Chapter V (4), whose role is to manage the fund for compensation and reparations to be paid to the victims and/or their families.

I remember Nhial Deng arguing that the process would be prone to abuse and that instead, the funds should be channeled to "the reconstruction of the infrastructure and rebuilding of livelihoods of communities in the states most affected by the conflict." He cites impracticalities of the same model in Sierra Leone, South Africa, Liberia, and Rwanda.

That is obviously prejudicial. The mere fact that a policy initiative failed elsewhere does not mean that it would also fail in South Sudan. Circumstances and contexts differ. In truth, the cited cases of Sierra Leone, South Africa, Liberia, and Rwanda should present a golden opportunity for South Sudan to draw lessons from said failures and develop a unique model that can be practical, fair and workable. The success of such initiatives is largely dependent upon the political will of the leadership group.

In the case of South Sudan, the problem is that there is no political will to make peace a reality. Moreover, the idea of compensating victims of war atrocities is probably too progressive for the government.

There are obligations easily derived from declarations such as the Declaration of Basic Principles of Justice for Victims of Crime and Abuse of Power (1985); the Convention against Torture and other Cruel, Inhuman or Degrading Treatment or Punishment (1984) and the Convention on the Prevention and Punishment of the Crime of Genocide (1948). A compensation program could be easily achieved.

As far as we know, Kiir's prioritization regarding infrastructure reconstruction and rebuilding the livelihoods of the South Sudanese people was a diversionary ploy to underplay and discount the merits of the compensation and reparation scheme. In any case, those two are the most essential elements of transitional justice, national healing, and reconciliation. They are key aspects in any post-conflict situation.

The truth of the matter is that Kiir and his cronies in his peace delegation, were not in favor of transitional justice in the first place.

I vividly remember Michael Lueth lamenting that it should start from 1991 and/or 2005 to cover the Bor Massacre. I responded by bringing it to Makuei's attention that the 1991 Bor atrocities were preceded by 1985 Gajaak Nuer massacre. I added that if we did that, we should then go all the way back to the time when John Garang and Salva Kiir himself were in command of those and other atrocities.

With their selective memories, they tend to forget that the SPLM/A under John Garang had committed atrocities in Nuer, Murle, Mundari, Didinga and Toposa lands.

There were also status reservations on the two vice presidents. Kiir preferred equal status. He argued that having a first vice president and a second vice president would be "a reward for rebellion" and "a humiliation to Second Vice President Igga, and his constituency, and that it had the potential to cause more problems across South Sudan."

He further objected to the power-sharing ratios proposed for the State Council of Ministers in Unity, Jonglei and Upper Nile states, as well as the nomination of governors from Kiir's Government of the Republic of South Sudan (GRSS), Machar's South Sudan Armed Opposition (SSAO), Amum's Former Detainees (FDs), and other political parties he collectively referred to as "rebels".

It is important to note Kiir's persistent use of the term "rebels" in reference to leaders who would be his partners in government to implement the peace agreement they signed with him. This could be easily interpreted as being against the spirit of reconciliation, which could create a lack of cooperation within the Transitional Government of National Unity (TGoNU).

In truth, none of Kiir's reservations were either reasonable or valid as they were all motivated by his very evident intransigence. This attitude turned the peace talks into protracted war talks. No amount of dialogue could help anyone to discern reservations motivated by the desire to retain power. The claim of his concerns to protect the "sovereignty and territorial integrity" of South Sudan were unfounded. Kiir's tribal army has never been used for the defense of the nation. It is always used for killing the nation.

Psychologically, SPLA is a symbol of trauma and genocide. That is why we have emphasized demilitarization of the major centers, thus allowing the people to return home.

When closely studying Kiir's reservations, one can easily see that he was still in a fighting mood. As he publicly stated, signing a document does not mean agreeing with its content and implementing it as you might think. If we reflect on his earlier statement that the agreement was neither a Holy Bible nor Holy Quran, it all makes sense when we take it in its proper context. It is an infamous quote of Sudan's former President Numeri to justify his abrogation of the 1972 Addis Ababa Agreement.

During the year that followed the signing, I gave those who believed in Kiir's desire to implement it a chance to achieve their vision vis-à-vis the unity of the SPLM and people of South Sudan. Nonetheless, it was always clear to me that Kiir was not serious about implementation, and that war was imminent. Our nascent state faced disintegration as long as that man remained in power.

Time has unfortunately proven me correct. In August 2016, Salva Kiir scrapped the Arusha Accords to unify the SPLM, and the Addis Ababa agreement to restore peace in South Sudan. Based on his statements, Kiir clearly adopted strategic positions against peace, the SPLM's unity, and returning to its vision. This is why I preferred my struggle in life as an exile and a political refugee. I continue struggling from there. My frustrating experiences negotiating with Kiir's regime from Addis Ababa to Juba during the advance missions convinced me beyond any reasonable doubt that South Sudan will never attain lasting peace and stability under his rogue regime.

Refer to Chapter VII (2.7) of ARCSS re the role of CTSAMM and Joint Monitoring and Evaluation Commission (JMEC).

Kiir's reservations on the roles and functions of the JMEC are in accordance with Chapter VII (3) of ARCSS.

CHAPTER TWELVE

Preparations for the Lion's Den

U pon the ratification of ARCSS by the SPLM (IO) National Liberation Council in Pagak, the movement embarked on political and security preparations for the return to Juba.

The first leadership meeting resolved to send a team of robust political and military cadres for trust building, dissemination security assessment, mobilization and reception of the leadership upon return to the national capital. The resolution proposed a multi-disciplinary team with expertise in various fields and strong mission support elements. The security team then embarked on setting the criteria for the force to be sent to Juba as JIU and police units.

General James Koang Chol impressed me with the criteria he set for the JIU soldiers as follows: "The soldier going to Juba must be at least 25 years old, an experienced combatant, literate, a well-known sniper tested in fire, knows the terrain of Juba and is not a drunkard."

This prompted me to consider similar rules for our security details co-opted into my reception and mobilization committee as protocol, logistic, media and information teams. We then set the criteria as: A high school or college graduate with security and military background or proven experience as a civil servant in the Government of South Sudan, the UN, a private sector or NGOs' world.

Those documents guided us well to select a competent team of highly educated young officers. As I came to know later on some of those officers previously served within Akol Koor's Special Branch (later converted into National Security). We then submitted the list

to the SPLA (IO) Military Intelligence Office in Pagak for further
scrutiny.

This three-month preparation period in Pagak was euphoric and
politically charged. The movement was overwhelmed by politicking
for positions in the forthcoming TGoNU. Unfortunately, strategic
thinking evaporated into the thinning air of false hope for lasting
peace and stability in the country. It was a politically charged
moment in time. One in which an extraordinary convention to elect
the members of the National Liberation Council and selection of
the advance team members took place.

It was a time well remembered for wrestling and wrangling over
the potential dividend of ARCSS. During intense debate under a
shady tented Hardeep tree, the majority wanted to return to Juba.
Various committees and clusters were formed to deal with the
challenges ahead. I was assigned to the governance committee
under Cde. Lado Gore, the Deputy Chairman of the SPLM (IO).

I served in that committee as the Secretary. My role was to
draft the key documents such as the portfolio selection matrix, the
terms of reference for the advance mission to Juba and the unified
political message. Those documents were presented at the Political
Bureau meeting for ratification and approval. I was also charged
with drafting the structure of the advance teams, which I presented
and was approved.

The Security Committee under General CDR James Koang
Chol presented the proposal at their meeting. It was a very busy
time for all the members of the movement. The SPLM/A (IO)
advance team was ready to travel to Juba by mid-November 2015.
While we were busy preparing the movement for return to Juba, we
received a shocking letter from the government's acting chief negotiator, Honorable Michael Makuei Lueth.. The letter was addressed
to the SPLM (IO) chief negotiator, Taban Deng Gai, and the leader
of FDs Pagan Amum Okiech

It read:

"Reference to the "Outcome of the Meeting of the Principal Signatory Parties to the Agreement on Planning Implementation of the Provisions in Chapter II of the Agreement (21 October to 3 November, 2015); this is to inform you (SPLM-IO and former detainees) that the Government of the Republic of South Sudan (GRSS) is yet to conclude preparations for the arrival of your respective advance teams by the middle of November 2015. Instead, we shall conclude all the necessary preparations by the 26th of November 2015," "In the meantime, we request that you kindly make available to us the full list of members of your respective advance teams expected in Juba by the 26th of November 2015".

This provoked a lot of debate in Pagak. Everyone was questioning the seriousness of the regime to implement the peace agreement. The SPLM-IO leadership also expected President Kiir to revoke his order creating the 'illegal' 28 states before the advance team traveled to Juba. They did not want it to become an obstacle to the implementation of an agreement signed on the basis of there being 10 states.

Dr. Machar made it very clear that it would be a waste of time and the lives of the movement's cadres to go to the lion's den without a prior meeting with Kiir outside of South Sudan. However, the growing desire of all to return to Juba overrode him after a series of lengthy debates.

There was an overwhelming fear of sanctions should the SPLM (IO) be seen as backtracking from the implementation process. President Festus Mogea, the former president of Botswana, who was tasked with the responsibility as the Chairman of JMEC to oversee the implementation of the peace agreement, had just visited Machar in Pagak. He urged him to speed up the return to

Juba and launch the JMEC in his presence. Dr Machar told him to go there first and establish JMEC in Juba.

Another difficulty facing JMEC was the attitude of the government. They declined to welcome the SPLM (IO) Advance Team. It was not clear why the government chose to delay preparations at this important stage. Sources close to the decision-making process confided that there appeared to be disagreements among the government's inner circle on how to handle the matter. Those who were initially against ARCSS wanted to frustrate the process. However, some in the government saw it as a political blunder to block the return of the rebels to the national capital. Nhial Deng and Makuei also sent a letter to JMEC protesting their terms of reference. They demanded that they must be approved first by the IGAD Head of States Summit to use them. They were particularly opposed to Article 8 of that document which prescribed punitive measures against violators and spoilers.

The Departure and the Arrival of the Advance Team

The departure of the Sudan People's Liberation Movement (SPLM-IO) Advance Team under the leadership of General Taban Deng Gai, the Chief Negotiator and the Chairman of the National Committee for Peace and Reconciliation, was scheduled to leave Pagak via the Gambella Regional Airport in neighboring Ethiopia. From there they would be airlifted to Juba on Monday, December 21, 2015.

The first team was comprised of 150 young and strong cadres. Another 459 were scheduled to follow on different dates before the end of the year to make a total of 609.

The first group was mainly composed of members who were designated to represent the SPLM/A (IO) in various institutions established under the peace agreement, including support staff. A number of senior military generals from the Command Council including Lt. General James Koang Chol and General Gatkor Gatluak were among the first group.

The Minister of Finance and Economic Planning, David Deng Athorbei chaired the government's national committee for the reception of the advance team. Cde. Akol Paul Kordit was the spokesman. The arrival had been canceled many times in the past due to disagreements between Juba and Pagak.

While the SPLM (IO) wanted the 609 members to return to Juba and to other states in order to mobilize the population to support the full implementation of the peace deal, the government wanted less than 50 of them, saying the "huge number" constituted a security risk and as a result added to the delays.

Fortuitously, with the intervention of Mr. Mogae the government finally agreed to receive the full number.

Upon arrival at Juba airport at around 10:30 PM, we held a press conference at the VIP Lounge. We then moved to the mausoleum of the late Dr. John Garang to pay our respects. According to the initial itinerary, we were supposed to visit SPLM House before finally going to the hotels where we were to be accommodated. However, that was canceled because of the late arrival.

The parties were now expected to jump-start the implementation of the first phases of the peace agreement. This was to include the deployment of joint integrated forces in Juba, constitutional amendments, selections of ministerial portfolios, designating of ministers and additional members to the national parliament, as well as the formation of a transitional government of national unity. It was all to be accomplished by January 22, 2016. Part of our terms of reference was to prepare for the reception of our Chairman, Dr. Machar. He was expected to return to Juba by then to form a TGoNU. All did not go according to plan.

Instead, the SPLA (IO) Chief of General Staff (COGS), 1st Lt. General Simon Gatwech Dual arrived in the morning of April 21. Five days later at 3:30 in the afternoon, Dr. Machar and his team arrived.

That was my prime responsibility as the Head of Mobilization and Reception Committee. Unfortunately, there was no adequate political space to do the things required. The NSC officers heavily guarded us and scrutinized everything we were doing. The itineraries we put in place to show that peace had returned to the country were canceled by General Boor Philip of National Security in the Office of the President.

Our movements within the city were strictly limited. We were technically detained at every opportunity. Exiting Juba without permission was prohibited. There was 24 hours' notice to be given prior to allowing any of us to leave the country. We were told that Salva Kiir himself was the one who signed off on these requests.

We were invited to the first State Christmas Dinner on December 26, 2016, at J1. While there, Kiir spent the time verbally attacking Machar and the SPLM (IO). As usual, he continued to chase the coup narrative. He again warned that the idea of taking the people's power by force must be abandoned. I reached the conclusion that peace was still a very distant possibility.

The Status of ARCSS Implementation

Since the signing of ARCSS, there were calls from both the region and the international community questioning the slow pace at which the deal was being implemented. Reports authored by Mr. Mogae, specifically warned of the political stalemate two weeks before the outbreak of violence in Juba: "I regret to report that the progress I had expected has not materialized. It leaves us with no option but to suspect that perhaps there is a serious lack of commitment towards peace. This deliberate and institutionalized impediment to the implementation of the agreement is totally unacceptable."

At a subsequent meeting in Khartoum of the agreement's guarantors on July 31, he stated: "We know that the forces of both parties and others allied to them continue to clash throughout the country, with a likelihood of larger battles increasing every day."

The formation of the TGoNU in April 2016 came with delays, maneuvers to undermine ARCSS, and visible tensions regarding the implementation of political and security arrangements. Reacting to his reservations, Kiir appointed and inaugurated the governors of his 28 states just two days after the arrival of the advance team.

We were shocked. We had to return to Pagak for consultation that divided the movement even further. The leadership in Pagak started to suspect that the advance team struck secret deals with Juba, especially on the 28 states. The movement could not decide which way to go.

The forced consensus was that we maintain to push for the abrogation of Kiir's 28 states, as they had become an obstacle to amending the Transitional Constitution of South Sudan, 2011.

Getting Dr. Machar to Juba was extremely difficult. That gave me weeks of sleepless nights. We had to set up an operations room to prepare for the reception of our Chairman. As previously stated, all of my proposed itineraries were canceled. There was little hope for projecting a popular and colorful return of Machar as a hero.

My billboards symbolizing the preparation for the return of our Chairman were often brought down at night by Kiir's National Security. They even included pictures of President Kiir and Dr. Machar posed together as peacemakers. My team and I were physically and verbally intimidated. This abuse was highlighted during the reception of Cde. Lado Gore whose itinerary, including his scheduled prayers at the Jubex Memorial site, was canceled by General Boor Philip.

Members of my information and media team were detained while announcing the tentative date for the arrival of the Chairman near the NCS building in Jabel. Prior to Machar's arrival, we had to bring the total force of 3,910 soldiers for both the JIU and the Police to Juba with their weapons. This was the most hectic part of the process.

The UN and the US totally refused to facilitate transportation of organic weapons like RPGs and PKMs. That was where we smelt a rat. The US Ambassador in particular, opposed transportation of our weaponss in all JMEC meetings. The government, to their credit, told the UN, and US that those actually were the organic weapons of the forces and they must bring them. Nhial spoke very well on that as a former minister of defense.

The American and UNIMISS representatives refused. I had to consult with the Ethiopian Ambassador, Mr Fesseh Shewel to help us out. In the end, he was successful.

The NSC took advantage of the UN and US position to refuse to allow in the total force of 3,000 troops of the SPLA (IO) JIU and the police force units in accordance with the Transitional Security Arrangement Agreement. The NSC went with CTSAM to inspect the SPLA (IO) weapons at the Gambella Regional Airport. This was not done in accordance with the agreement, but General Taban seemed not to care very much about that.

Some real threats were made by high figures in the government. General Kuol Manyang, the Minister of Defense spoke on public record during the graduation ceremony of military police officers and stated that Riek Machar would not escape this time around if he continued with his deadly ambition of taking the people's power by force. This was widely seen in the media. We wrote a protest letter, but it was all in vain.

National Security went so far as refusing to permit Dr. Machar's plane into South Sudanese airspace while it was en route to Juba. He and his entourage were stranded in Gambella for days.

Generally speaking, there was a lack of progress re implementation and a violation of prior agreements. Most notably these were; the Cessation of Hostilities Agreement; the Agreement to Resolve the Crisis in South Sudan; and the Areas of Agreement on the Establishment of the Transitional Government of National Unity in the Republic of South Sudan. We were not moving as fast on the key provisions and stipulation of ARCSS as hoped. Even the implementation of the Arusha Agreement on Reunification of the SPLM was moribund.

As a Focal-Point Person for the implementation of the Arusha Agreement, I suffered the humiliating gestures of Madam Nunu Kembe, the Acting Secretary General of the SPLM (IG). She acted as if there wasn't even an agreement to be implemented. She violated Article 19 of the Arusha Agreement, which stipulates that: "All the processes of holding a national convention shall be suspended until the reunification and reconciliation of the party are achieved and the war is ended so that all members are able to take part in the convention. She and her team went ahead to schedule an Extraordinary Convention to pass SPLM documents in violation of the agreement.

We then reached a dead end on the implementation of the Arusha Accord. Whether on the Addis Ababa or Arusha track, we failed to move an inch. In stead of driving on the same wavelength to implement the two agreements, the government was busy broadcasting its reservations on ARCSS and consolidating its powers. They wanted to scrap every agreement we ever signed with them.

The only thing the parties accomplished was the appointment of Dr. Machar as the First Vice President and constituting the Council of Ministers in April 2016. This was provided for in ARCSS when forming the TGoNU. From there, the parties began establishing the necessary institutions of governance.

However, the implementation of other provisions in ARCSS had been slow. There was a lack of progress on the formation of the Transitional National Legislative Assembly (TNLA) through the expansion of the existing 300-member National Legislative Assembly by an additional 68 members as provided for under Chapter I (11) of ARCSS.

Representing the SPLM (IO), I had the advantage of attending some major meetings of JMEC and had the opportunity to listen to the reports. They stated that there were key disagreements on the selection of the speaker of the TNLA, a lack of consensus over the appointment of presidential advisors and a lack of progress with regard to reviewing the 28 state problem. Kiir, when discussing the additional states, proclaimed they were for the purpose of: "Devolving power and bringing resources closer to the people, reducing government expenditure and promoting development."

However, the decision had been criticized as a veiled attempt by Kiir's regime to grab the Upper Nile and Bahr el Ghazal to annex them to Dinka lands.

CTSAMM, with the mandate provided for under Chapter II (4) of ARCSS of monitoring compliance and reporting to JMEC on the implementation progress of PCTSA, had been facing restrictions in doing its work. Concurrently, humanitarian deliveries were report-edly being obstructed in Western Equatoria and Northern Bahr el Ghazal.

There were reports that CTSAMM monitoring and verification teams in areas such as Yambio, Torit, and Juba were being intimi-dated and restricted in terms of carrying out their operations. Some local authorities were demanding to see presidential authority before any access was granted.

Government departments and offices within TGoNU appeared to be disjointed. Kiir did a lot of prior restructuring and reshuffling in the ministries to be given to the opposition. This was one of the most serious challenges for incumbent opposition ministers. It further complicated matters for TGoNU to forge interparty trust, consultation, communication, cooperation, dialogue, and consensus.

For example, Machar and Igga issued a joint press statement on June 1, 2016 to the effect that the South Sudan's presidency (comprising those two and Kiir) had agreed to review the 28 states through a 15-member committee, constituted by 10 South Sudanese and 5 representatives from the international partners.

However, on June 3, Honorable Tor Deng Mawien, a senior advisor to Kiir on decentralization and intergovernmental linkages, dismissed the press statement whilst denying that consensus had been reached to review the states.

The slow implementation of ARCSS was also evidenced by the delays in the formation and reconstitution of transitional institutions and mechanisms provided for under Chapter I (14.1) of the agreement. This included inter alia, the Peace Commission (PC); Relief and Rehabilitation Commission (RRC); Refugees Commission (RC) and other institutions such as the Commission for Truth, Reconciliation and Healing (CTRH), the Hybrid Court for South Sudan (HCSS), CRA, and the Board of the Special Reconstruction Fund (BSRF).

All these had not yet been established, yet most were supposed to be in place within the first month of the TGoNU as provided for in ARCSS. With respect to the National Architecture and Joint Military Ceasefire Commission, the JMEC has also reported that the Joint Military Ceasefire Commission (JMCC), whose mandate under Chapter I (3.3) was to oversee and coordinate forces in cantonments and barracks, was not fully operational as its chair was distracted by other commitments.

In addition, the Strategic Defense and Security Review Board (SDSRB) was not carrying out its work. Its stated excuse was that it failed to reach a quorum with other security institutions such as the Joint Integrated Police (JIP), Joint Operations Centre (JOC) and the Joint Military Ceasefire Team (JMCT). The SDSRB was also failing to perform its functions due to a shortage of working space, and a lack of transport and communication essentials.

However, President Mogae, as chair of the JMEC, dismissed the explanation that these institutions were failing to operate due to funding shortages, arguing that there was no political will. He also noted that the JMCC's failure to meet and work as a team "impeded the integration of forces". This resulted in the widespread violence committed by members of the Shilluk and Dinka communities in Malakal, that culminated in the death of 18 people and injuries to 50 others in February 2016.

Again, in March of that year, there was reported violence in Western Equatoria, Central Equatoria, Western Bahr el Ghazal, Malakal, and the Upper Nile states. UN Secretary-General Ban Ki-moon expressed his concern over the fighting between the SPLM/A (IG) and SPLM/A (IO) in Juba, Wau, and Bentiu, as well as reported attacks on UN and humanitarian operations.

Due to the reported violence and hostilities in most parts of South Sudan, in March 2016 Ban Ki-moon urged the warring parties to "rebuild mutual trust and confidence from the people and the international community to set the country on a path to stability." He further implored the South Sudanese leaders to; "put peace above politics" through compromise, so as to bring stability. This did not deter Kiir from implementing his plans to serve as a power base for the national elites.

The Last Rain

In Salva Kiir tradition from the SPLM/A bush days, political and security rumors in the form of plots or coup attempts can be processed and made out to be real events. So, most political and security rumors are true in Juba. The code name for the July 2016 Crisis was rumored to us as "The Last Rain" upon our arrival in Juba.

To Kiir's hoodlums, this would be the last war. One in which Riek Machar and his SPLM (IO) leaders would be killed and that this would be the last rain of bullets. The conflict would be settled militarily much like the scenario that unfolded with UNITA and the MPLA in Angola. Their assessment was that with just 1,370 troops, Riek and his leadership would not escape this time around.

The cantonment of forces 25 kilometers from Juba became the active military strategy to siege it by closing all the routes out to the other states. The fascist regime then started mounting roadblocks throughout the city to close in Machar and the SPLA (IO).

To provide the needed spark to ignite the crisis, the SPLA Military Intelligent (MI) units began hostile actions on July 2, 2016, with the killing of two SPLA (IO) military officers, Colonel George Gismala and Lieutenant Colonel Domach Koat Pinyien. Three days later, a confrontation between the SPLA (IO) and SPLA soldiers at a checkpoint resulted in the killing of five SPLA soldiers.

The conflict quickly escalated. On July 6, while the president and the two vice presidents were meeting at State House, heavy gunfire erupted outside the building and quickly spread to other areas of Juba. Fighting resumed on the 8th and continued through the 9th, 10th, and 11th throughout Juba. The SPLA attacked SPLM (IO) cantonment areas in Jebel and the residence of First Vice-President Machar. The result was over 300 deaths, the displacement of 40,000 people, attacks on civilians and on United Nations Protection of Civilians sites. Two peacekeepers were killed and there was mass looting.

Versions of those events and trigger points differ. Each party accused the other of political and military wrongdoing. The most likely explanation is what one local media outlet quoted military sources as stating. "That the SPLA attacked the SPLA (IO) vice-presidential guards as revenge for the killing of the five soldiers the day before." That is what Thomas Duoth of National Security alluded to when he said: "Bringing Gatluak Thian and Riew Manguet to J1 ignited the crisis."

A UN memo stated that: "A huge force came out of nowhere and joined up with the President's Tiger Force. They opened fire on Machar's bodyguards deployed outside the palace for protection."

According to the government version, it was a coup attempt initiated by SPLA (IO) Lieutenant Colonel David Riew Manguet.

Kiir's hoodlums also blamed SPLM (IO) spokesman James Gatdet Dak for instigating the conflict with a post on social media claiming that Machar was being detained in the Presidency right after the initial shots were fired on July 6. For sure, they said, it was an assassination attempt.

On the 9th of July, Dr. Machar called upon UNIMISS to create a buffer zone manned by a neutral third force to monitor the declared ceasefire.

Another conspiracy theory of the 'last rain' was that it was all a planned coup against the TGoNU involving collusion between SPLM (IO) Mining Minister General Taban Deng Gai; General Paul Malong, the SPLA Chief of General Staff, and President Kiir.

The deployment of MI-24 attack helicopters and ground forces on July 10 verified that there was a premeditated manhunt for Dr. Machar under the direct command and control of the President and Commander in Chief.

Remember that Salva Kiir once said that the ongoing war in Wau would come to Juba sooner or later. He was referring to the clashes between the SPLA (IO) and the SPLA forces in Western Bar-El-Ghazal at that time due to the violation of the Permanent Ceasefire Agreement (PCA) as stipulated in ARCSS.

On July 11, fighting erupted in other areas of the country, including Torit, Wau and Upper Nile. SPLA units spent weeks in hot pursuit of Machar and his entourage in Central and Western Equatoria. Senior Equatorian leaders stated that their militias and rebel groups helped defend Machar. Then, fully understanding that they too would not be spared by the government forces, they entered the Democratic Republic of Congo and were extracted to safety by the UN Mission several weeks later.

A few days after Machar's departure from Juba, Kiir appointed Taban Deng to replace him as First Vice president. Machar's faction of the SPLM (IO) called the appointment illegal and a violation of ARCSS as Taban Deng had been relieved of his ministerial portfolio and his party membership. However, Taban Deng's SPLM(IO) faction, or the Crown Hotel Grouping as we call them, said the appointment was necessary after Machar's departure from Juba in order for TGoNU to continue implementing the peace accord.

A ceasefire was declared on July 11. In response, IGAD and the AU called for the deployment of a regional force with a more robust mandate than the 12,000-strong UNMISS.

CHAPTER THIRTEEN

All Agreements Dishonored

" *ARCSS is neither a Gospel nor Holy Qur'an"*
Salva Kiir Mayardit

The Southern Sudanese political leaders and intellectuals had always been bitter about the Northern Sudanese regimes in Khartoum for dishonoring agreements throughout the history of north-south conflict. One of the most renowned South Sudanese political science scholars, Dr. Dustain Wai, documented them in his book entitled: *The Afro-Arab Conflict in Sudan.*

The former Chairman of the High Executive Council for South Sudan and Vice President of the Republic of Sudan, the Honorable Abel Alier also chronicles the problem in his book: *Southern Sudan: Too Many Agreements Dishonored.* He observed that "the provisions of the agreements we signed with Khartoum were quite satisfactory on paper and could have gone a long way to meet the complaints of the South, but none of the parties believed they would be implemented!"

Comparing and contrasting those historical accounts with current political affairs under the Jieng (JCE) State in Juba, we can say with ease that we have inherited the worst part of the Jalaba state: *One that does not only dishonor some agreements but all agreements.*

I could not believe my ears to I hear Salva Kiir parroting President Jaffer Numeri policy he rebelled against in 1983 for dishonouring Addiss-Ababa Agreement. True to his word, Salva Kiir signed many agreements with the SPLM (IO) and implemented only one ; the Agreement on the status of the ten detainees (G10 /FDS). Other than that, the five year long IGAD peace process produced the following signed agreements, all of which were dishonored:

▌ Agreement on Cessation of Hostilities (CoH) and its Humanitarian Component, January 23, 2014.
▌ Agreement on the Status of Detainees January 23, 2014.
▌ Recommitment to Humanitarian Matters of Agreement on Cessation of Hostilities (CoH) May 5, 2014.
▌ Agreement on Political Framework on the Resolution of Conflict in South Sudan May 9, 2014.
▌ Re-Dedication of and Implementation Modalities for Cessation of Hostilities (CoH) Agreement November 9, 2014.
▌ Agreement on the Reunification of the SPLM January 21, 2015 in Arusha, Tanzania;
▌ The Agreement on the Resolutions of Conflict in the Republic of South Sudan (ARCSS) August 17, 2015.
▌ The Cessation of Hostilities Agreement on Humanitarian Access and Protection of Civilians on December 22, 2017.

In its effort to implement the signed agreement, the leadership of the SPLM/SPLA (IO) did the following:

▌ Announced Declaration of Cessation of Hostilities (CoH) and a Permanent Ceasefire within 72 hours after the signing of ARCSS and embarked on disengagements, separation, and withdrawal of its forces from contested areas.
▌ The National Liberation Council (NLC) of the SPLM/SPLA (IO) ratified the Agreement within a week pursuant to its provision.
▌ The SPLM/SPLA (IO), for the purpose of peace implementa-tion, dispatched the first batch of its Advanced Team to Juba

on December 20, 2015. The first contingent of its joint force arrived Juba on March 30, 2016. The remaining top leaders including Dr. Machar, arrived on April 26, 2016. He was sworn in on the same day as First Vice President of TGoNU. The leadership of SPLM/SPLA (IO) assigned ten ministers, two Deputy Ministers in the executive of TGoNU; fifty members of Transitional National Legislative Assembly (TNLA); and assigned members to the JMEC, CTSAMM, JMCC, SDSR, JOC, etc. bodies for the implementation of the agreement.

The Major Violations that Rendered ARCSS Collapsed

Pursuant to Chapter VIII Articles 3 & 4, ARCSS is the supreme law of the land with legal force to prevail over any legislation.

Unfortunately, with the systemic violation by Kiir's regime from day one, it became impractical to implement the agreement following the assassination attempt on the life of the First Vice President on July 8, 2016, in the Presidential Palace. While under heavy ground and aerial attacks from July 10, 2016, to August 16, 2017, the leadership of the SPLM/SPLA (IO) withdrew from their defensive position in Juba. For ease of reference, the major violations that rendered the agreement obsolete are outlined as follows:

▌ In gross violation of Article 1(1.1.6, 15.2 & 15.3) of ARCSS, President Salva Kiir issued order 36 to create 28 states on Friday 2nd October 2015.

▌ In violation of the article cited afore and in defiance of the worldwide condemnation, President Salva Kiir appointed governors to his 28 states on December 23, 2015, two days after the first SPLM (IO) peace advance team arrived in Juba.

▌ Persistent violations of Article 5 (5.2,5 & 1.1.3) of ARCSS re the permanent cease fire within 48 hours of its declaration, through multiple attacks on SPLA (IO) positions in Leer, Mayendit and Koch counties in Southern Unity State.

▌ As outlined in its list of 16 reservations, the regime deliberately violated the provisions on demilitarization of Juba and relocation of troops to the radius of 25 km within 90 days from the day of the signing of the Agreement as stipulated in Article 5 (5.1).

▌ Instead of demilitarizing Juba, the regime embarked on serious militarization of the town by deploying more forces. In total twenty-five thousand were deployed there.

▌ In blatant violation of Article (4.1, 4.2) of ARCSS on the Transitional Security Arrangement, the regime continued to deny the Cease-fire Transitional Security Monitoring Mechanism (CTSAMM) teams access for monitoring and to carry out their mandate as per the Agreement. Members of CTSAMM faced intimidation, harassment, and arbitrary detention.

▌ A comprehensive report submitted to the UN by the Chairman of JMEC President Festus Mogai on June 23, 2016, clearly stated the multiple violations by the regime.

▌ The SPLA (IG) continued attacking the SPLA (IO) cantonment sites particularly in the regions of Equatoria, Bahr el Ghazal. This was in violation of Article 1 (1.1,1.2 &1.3) regarding the permanent ceasefire and the containment of forces.

▌ Kiir appointed advisers to the Presidency without consultation with the First Vice President on Wednesday, May 4, 2016, in violation of the power-sharing agreement stipulated in Article 8 (8.1.1).

▌ The mounting of security checkpoints along the road leading to the residence of the FVP to harass and intimidate members of SPLM/A (IO), which is also in violation of Article 5 (5.1) regarding demilitarization of the capital.

▌ The refusal to lift the state of emergency in the country, which the president instituted December 15, 2013. It was a collegial and consultative power stipulated in Article 8 (8.2.1).

▌ The murder of two SPLM/SPLA (IO) officers by the regime military intelligence in Juba on July 2, 2016.

▌ The assassination attempt on the First Vice President in J1 on July 8th, 2016.

▌ The subsequent airstrikes on and the bulldozing of the residence of the First Vice President in Juba on July 10th & 11th, 2016.

▌ Violation of the cease-fire declared on July 11, 2016, by attacking the SPLM (IO) positions beginning July 13, 2016.

▌ The unilateral appointment of the Speaker of TNLA and dismissal of some MPs of the Transitional National Assembly violated Articles 1 (1.1.6, 15.2 & 15.3) of the Agreement on Conflict Resolution in South Sudan (ARCSS).

▌ Illegal replacement of the legitimate First Vice President Machar with General Taban Deng (who had ceased to be a member of the SPLM (IO)) at the time of his appointment. This was in violation of both Article 5 (5.3) and Article 6 (4) of ARCSS as well as the SPLM (IO) Constitution.

▌ The violent military pursuit for 40 days by the regime's ground forces, drones and helicopter gunships of the SPLM/SPLA (IO) leadership, who withdrew from Juba to the Democratic Republic of Congo after the July 12, 2016 aerial and ground attacks on them.

▌ The regime launched a scorched-earth campaign against unarmed civilians and targeted them based on ethnicity. They had committed acts of genocide, war crimes and crimes against humanity, particularly in Equatoria, Western Bahr el Ghazal and the Shilluk Kingdom since July 2016.

As he vowed to do in his document of reservations, President Kiir totally refused to implement the agreement he signed with the SPLM (IO) and other stakeholders. Subsequently, his cumulative and systematic flagrant violations of ARCSS rendered its implementation impossible. All this amidst continuous pressure from the citizens of the Republic of South Sudan who wanted peace.

The assassination attempts on the First Vice President on July 8, 2016, in Presidential Palace and the subsequent aerial and ground attacks on the leadership of SPLM/SPLA (IO) including members of Advance Team made the permanent ceasefire collapse under the watch of the guarantors. They managed a total failure to play their role as provided for in Article 2.3 of the agreement. Hence, ARCSS collapsed, and so did the ToGNU established by it.

The government's military expedition against the leadership of SPLM/A (IO), and attacks on their forces in Equatoria and Western Bhar el Ghazal, caused conflict to engulf the entire country. This led to massive death, destruction, and displacement of within and without.

Cessation of Hostilities Agreement Scrapped

The High-Level Revitalization Forum concluded its first phase with the signing of an Agreement on a Cessation of Hostilities, Protection of Civilians and Humanitarian Access. It was set to come into force at 00:01 hours (South Sudan local time) on the December 24, 2017 and was to set the stage for further discussions required for the revitalization process.

The IGAD Special Envoy for South Sudan, Ambassador Ismail Waise and the Co-Facilitators of the Forum, H.E. Ramtane Lamamra, H.E. Hanna Tetteh and H.E. George Rebelo Chicoti, announced the successful conclusion of Phase I.

They expressed their appreciation to the South Sudanese stakeholders, representatives of the government, opposition parties, armed and non-armed groups, as well as the representatives of civil society organizations, eminent persons, business, women, and youth. Upon the signing of the COH, Dr. Machar sent a circular to all the SPLA (IO) units to cease fire immediately, release all POWs and to act only in self-defense.

Unfortunately, as with all previous agreements, Kiir's regime violated every provision. Instead of reciprocating, he and his cronies did the opposite by killing our POWs and sentencing detainees and abductees to death. They continued to attack SPLA (IO) positions throughout the country.

They demonstrated their audacity by disregarding the CoH and pursuing both violence and the obstruction of peace. Kiir's delegation declined to sign the Declaration of Principles. They cited Article 28 of that document. It provided for punitive action against any party that obstructs or spoils the peace process during Phase II of the HLRF peace talks.

Curiously, instead of holding Kiir's regime responsible for violation of the COH, the IGAD Council of Foreign Ministers called upon Dr. Machar, who by their own admission was a political detainee in South Africa, to renounce violence as a precondition for his release.

This incriminating condition was meant to project the victim of violence and unfair detention as the sole violence maker in the country. This, when all evidence pointed directly at Kiir, who was totally exonerated from implication by IGAD's nonsensical approach.

It was all tantamount to a violation of the COH. The agreement provided for the release of all political detainees. Did this not include Dr. Machar, a political detainee of IGAD?

Machar was the one calling for peace. He wrote letters to many world leaders to resuscitate ARCSS culminating in the HRF. He continued with his relentless search for peace amidst military offensives by Kiir's regime up to and including the commencement of HRF. He supported this and sent a high-level delegation under the leadership of his deputy. The SPLM/A (IO) delegation to peace talks, Phase I of the HRF, signed a CoHA on December 22, 2017.

See Article 1 (1.1.6, 15.2 and 15.3) of ARCSS, President Salva Kiir issued Order #36 to create 28 states on Friday October 2, 2015 and appointed governors to them on December 23, 2015, two days after the arrival of first SPLM (IO) peace advance team arrived in Juba.

See Article 2.3 of ARCSS re the role of guarantors and Article (4.1, 4.2) on the Transitional Security Arrangement re the role of the Cease-fire Transitional Security Monitoring Mechanism (CTSAMM).

CHAPTER FOURTEEN

The Era of Lackluster Diplomacy

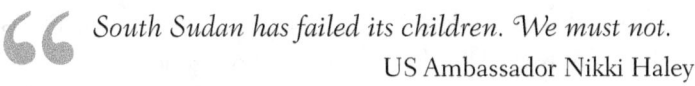 *South Sudan has failed its children. We must not.*
US Ambassador Nikki Haley

The diplomacy of war and peacemaking in South Sudan has ushered in a querulous language that tends to bash both sides of the conflict on equal measure. However, Kiir's regime has been blamed for most of the violations. "While both sides are responsible for atrocities against civilians, the government is primarily responsible for ethnically based killings" stated Ambassador Nicky Haley of the United States to the UN. She further stated that "Salva Kiir's regime has been engaging in a brutal, protracted military campaign against a fragmented armed opposition since July 2016." True, Salva Kiir's fascist regime had been taking advantage of the regionally coordinated policy of isolating the SPLM/A(IO) and the fragmentation of the armed opposition to win the war militarily.

"We are now blaming most of the atrocities on the govern- ment, which is what is happening in the latter part of this conflict," said Simona Foltyn, a South Sudan focused journalist and videographer.

Since then, condemnations have compiled volumes against the regime. From the AU Commission of Inquiry Report (AUCIR) of January 2015, to the UN Panel of Experts Reports of July 2016, to the EU and TROIKA statements against declaration of 28 states in violation of ARCSS in October 2015, the statements of TROIKA and the UN Panel of expert's testimony before the US Senate Foreign Relations Committee dated July 8, 2017. Considering those documents including human right reports as well as JMEC and CTSAM reports, the fault lines of the crisis in South Sudan could not be clearer. The verdict in the court of international public opinion is: Salva Kiir manufactured this crisis, financed it, committed genocide and scrapped ARCSS in the full view of the world. So far, the regime has been exposed and depicted as ethnocentric, genocidal, fascist, corrupt and rogue. Ironically, the authors of those reports failed to do anything practical to deter the regime's violent and militaristic attitude. Until the time of this writing the same international community still recognizes it as the legitimate custodian of South Sudan's sovereignty. Like all rogue regime, Kiir's regime is a survivalist by instinct.

Over time and space, the regime has developed skills to maneuver its way through tumultuous waters of war and diplomatic pressures. Evidently, it thrives and survives on the tunes of the hot air diplomacy. Subsequently, the rogue regime has gotten away with rape, mass murder and gross diplomatic hostilities including military attacks on US diplomats in their own CD registered vehicles.

Exploiting the existing impotent diplomacy of the West, Kiir's regime bought the necessary time to crush his shackled and diplomatically isolated opponents in South Sudan. Taking the world for a long ride, Salva Kiir used to say one thing and did completely the opposite. He would declare a unilateral ceasefire while launching a scorched-earth military offensive at the same time. Salva kiir signed ARCSS while posting 16 points of reservations to justify dishonoring it with straight face. Ironically he used the very agreement he dishonored to legitimize his junta dubbed TGoNU.

As ploys to buy legitimacy, Kiir used every trick in the book. True to form, he initiated a diversionary monologue sugarcoated as National Dialogue in the middle of a raging war to avoid any inclu- sive political process that might challenge his ill-gotten power and stolen legitimacy. In tandem with his allies in the region, the international community has been diplomatically black mailed with those gimmicks and face-saving projects such as High Revitalization Forum and the reunification of the SPLM under the patronage of his mentor, Yoweri Kaguta Museveni. Eventually, the regional and world leaders found themselves left in the cold of their own lackluster diplomacy. Confused by Kiir's regional allies, the positions of the AU, TROIKA and the UN on the resolution of South Sudanese conflict remained ambiguous.

Even the United States, which has always been the loudest voice against the excesses of Kiir's regime, has totally failed to develop a well-defined foreign policy for South Sudan and the region as things stand today. Although the Obama administra- tion acknowledged its own failures in South Sudan as it exited the White House, the people of South Sudan were left to fend for themselves amidst military offensives, famine, economic crises, mass displacement, genocides and death at the brutal hands of the well-known unknown gunmen in Juba. The decay of this diplomatic discourse is underscored by the gross injustice that the helpless victims at the receiving end are the ones being asked to denounce violence while the monster with the mightier means of violence is left to roam and roar without any fear of reprisal. In this diplomacy of empty threats of sanctions and arms embargoes, IGAD has been warning the warring parties that it would not tolerate any further violation of the cessation of hostilities agreement since 2014. This has been a consis- tent pattern since ARCSS negotiations right up to the HRF period. Overall, the tone has always been consistently loud and completely hollow.

Opening the first session the of the Phase II of High-level Revitalization forum on South Sudan, the Ethiopian Foreign Affairs Minister and the IGAD Council of Ministers Chairperson Dr. Workneh Gebeyehu told the delegations of South Sudan's warring parties that IGAD will not tolerate any further violation of the CoH agreement and is ready to take action against the two sides if they don't comply. "We are not saying this only for the sake of saying it!" he stressed.

On January 12, 2018 the Chairman of the African Union Commission and Dr. Workneh issued a joint statement condemning violations of the CoH and voicing the firm view that there must be consequences for parties violating it. On the same day, TROIKA and the US issued a similar statement condemning the continuing pattern of violations and stating their readiness to hold those responsible to account and to impose measures on those who violated the agreement.

On January 25, the IGAD Council of Ministers requested all parties to investigate and report within one month on violations and cases of sexual and gender-based violence and child recruitment and identify the individuals responsible.

Those condemnations were also echoed in statements by the European Union and TROIKA on January 26 & 29 respectively.

As if that was not enough, the African Union, IGAD and the United Nations jointly condemned and called for accountability for violations of the CoH and rejected threats directed towards the Ceasefire and Transitional Security Arrangements Monitoring Mechanism on January 27.

On the same date, the IGAD Council of Ministers issued a communiqué in which it endorsed the mechanism's verified violation reports and reaffirmed its commitment to take appropriate action, including targeted sanctions, against those violating the agreement.

Unfortunately due to the empty threats the lackluster diplomacy on the part of the western and regional countries, the regime got away with bizarre excesses and grew even more intransigent. In the process, they continued to drive South Sudan to the abyss. It is more evident now than ever that without tangible diplomatic heat, or extreme cold in the form of arms embargoes, coordinated sanctions and diplomatic isola- tion, Kiir will always have his way. To him, war is the surest way to cling to power. Another long overdue remedy is the establishment of the HCSS to investigate and prosecute individuals bearing criminal responsibility for war crime to halt the existing culture of impunity. As provided for in Transitional Justice of Protocol of ARCSS, the peace and reconciliation process run concurrently with justice and accountability under the Hybrid Court for South Sudan. However, the implementation of that provision requires a well-coordinated diplomatic effort that calls a spade a spade. First and foremost, the prevailing querulous language of bashing both sides must end as it simply sends a dangerous signal to Kiir's regime that inter- national community does not have the gut and gusto to threaten his existence. Otherwise, documentation has already indicted Salva Kiir and his cronies. It has been widely acknowledged that his regime bears the principal responsibility for the conflict, the troubled nature of peace negotiations, and the devastating suffering inflicted on millions South Sudanese. As the violent conflict stretched from weeks to months and to years, the people have remained in limbo where they are protected from their own government by UNMISS within their own cities. This simply means that the so-called national govern- ment has not only failed to carry out its prime function of public security but has also become a real threat to the lives of its own citizens. That is why we have been advocating for external intervention

The Juba regime opposes this in the name of protecting the sovereignty of the country but the hard truth is that if framed and implemented in the right manner, it can be used as a vehicle to help South Sudan become a functioning and responsive state worthy of existence. The world must also demonstrate it to this rogue regime that sovereignty without the responsibility to protect the citizens under international law, can only diminish as the conflict progresses.

According to Professor Idris Amir of Fordham University: "South Sudan cannot save itself. It needs to be saved from itself."

This means that the scope and severity of human suffering in South Sudan demands practical intervention by the United Nations, African Union and TROIKA. They must use their combined leverage on the key regional players such as Uganda, Kenya, Sudan, and Ethiopia. Only global forces can tell them that investing on Kiir's tyranny is not in the best interest of their own citizens who are bearing the brunt of this war in terms of hosting the refugees and trade impediments. In other words, it is time to make it very clear to Kiir and his allies in the region that resolving the crisis by might of arms is a perilous option. This time around, the international community must look to the interest of the people, not the almighty demigods in control of those garrisoned slum-towns. It is also crucial to listen to opposing political voices, civil society organizations, faith-based groups and other national stakeholders. Ultimately, the existing lackluster diplomacy must end. The decay of this diplomacy is amply demonstrated by the latest position of TROIKA on the peace process that they can not support another power-sharing agreement between Kiir's regime and the opposition.

Initially, the United States made it a point that it won't fund South Sudan's government or act as guarantor unless the peace process includes civil societies, churches, women, other excluded groups and that there is no longer a "narrow agreement between elites." Well, all the South Sudanese political forces have already signed the Revitalized Agreement on Conflict Resolution in South Sudan(R-ARCSS) along with all the nonpartisan groups including civil society organizations and the faith-based groups. The question here is what does the US want to do with a regime they have already declared rogue? Should it be regime change peace making with Kiir's regime? The question I put to one TROIKA diplomat to critique this mind-boggling position was: "How can a rogue regime with long history of dishonoring agreements implement this agreement without tangible pressure and the practical involvement of the international community?" I call it diplomacy of doing nothing by saying something. We can be diplomatic about it but the ugly truth is that the United Nations and TROIKA' are failing the children of South Sudan the same way South Sudan has failed her own children in betrayal of what Ambassador Haley promised. Ultimately, the United States must match its diplomatic rhetoric with tangible actions on the ground in South Sudan. The United States and its western allies must also remember that there are no other powers in the world with their leverage on the key states in this region to end this humanly devastating conflict. It goes without informing the records that the current engagement with the region contradicts the policy declaration made in by Donald Y. Yamamoto in September 2017. The following letter was my response to that declaration.

Open Letter to Ambassador Donald Y. Yamamoto

The Principal Deputy Assistant Secretary, Bureau of African Affairs

US Department of State, Washington, D.C. September 21, 2017

by Stephen Par Kuol

Your Excellency Ambassador Yamamoto:
It gives me profound pleasure to register to Your Excellency that you have made my day with your presentation at U.S. Peace Institute on September 13, 2017. The document entitled, Partnership with Africa: Advancing the Common Interest is timely, diplomatically strong and extremely encouraging. Among other critical issues, my take-home delicacy was the official pronouncement that the U.S. partnership with Africa is now mandatorily geared toward working with "strong institutions, and not with dictators or strong men in the continent." Being a policy statement by the top diplomat and expert on African affairs in the State Department, it is expressly inferred as an historic point of departure from the existing unwritten policy, which is inherently fraught with consistent lack of statesmanship, double standards and a gross disposition to shun the very core values of American freedom and democracy.
That disastrous policy has been implemented in South Sudan where Kiir's ethnocentric fascist regime has been using American taxpayers' money to build sectarian institutions committing heinous atrocities against both South Sudanese and the U.S. citizens working in South Sudan. The Terrain Hotel savagery of July 2016 where American aid workers were gang raped, the barbaric attack on the U.S. diplomatic vehicle (CD) carrying American diplomats by none other than Kiir's own bodyguard and

the recent murder of Christopher Allen, the American journalist they derogatorily profiled as a white rebel are just few examples of those humiliating provocations in the treacherous bilateral relations between Juba and Washington D.C. In betrayal of those American souls, the U.S. diplomats still dine and waltz with those cheeky diplomats of Kiir's regime without any qualm in Juba, New York, D.C. and all other world capitals. That does not sound like the United States of America I have known so far!

As exposed by Secretary Kerry's recent haste to bless the systematically rigged elections in Kenya, the ordinary Africans have concluded that the U.S. love affair with dictatorship in the continent is matched only by its hate for the very democratic principles it claims to promote. I was stunned to see John Kerry scrupulously apologizing to Honorable Raila Odinga for endorsing election results that robbed him of his rightful victory. I think John Kerry needs to do the same to Dr. Riek Machar, the champion of ARCSS whom they have arbitrarily exiled in South Africa and the people of South Sudan he condemned to famine, displacement and mass-murder by the junta he legitimized in violation of the Agreement on Resolution of the Conflict in South Sudan (ARCSS) which cost U.S. taxpayers millions of US dollars to sponsor in Addis Ababa.

Ambassador Yamamoto, as a practiced diplomat in the continent, you know that the United States of America has been and is still putting its biggest bet on the strong men of Africa. In pursuit of such a decayed policy, the United States is still doing business with a murderous police state that has reduced civic and democratic forces to an endangered species. From the Horn to the Great Lakes, the former heads of rebel movements turned heads of states are running their fragile states with iron fists. With the diplomatic weight of the United States behind them, they have cowed all the democratic political forces in their countries either to servitude or pushed them to armed uprising as in the case of South Sudan.

Ambassador Yamamoto, as you articulated in the sub-title of your eloquent presentation, (Advancing the Common Interest), diplomatic relations are naturally driven by mutual interests of the states in question. In your case, it is obvious that the most vital strategic interest of the U.S. in the Horn of Africa at the moment is counterterrorism and that is what the U.S. love affair with some dictators in the region is based on. Their opportunistic vow to fight Al-Shabab in Somalia gives false sense of security for the U.S. strategic interest in the region. Well, experiences in the continent have proven that African dictators can give a false appearance of order and stability while in reality sowing the seeds of present and future destabilization. In truth, those despots are responsible for all the armed conflicts in the continent. One good example is the Somalia itself that was wrecked to pieces by dictator Mohamed Siad Barre. Another example is the nascent Republic of South Sudan, which is now being pushed to the precipice of disintegration by its dictator, Salva Kiir.

In any case, the new strings attached to partnership with Africa are encouraging. Unfortunately, dictators naturally loathe institutionalism and the rule of law to provide a conducive geopolitical environment for the underlined four pillars of your new policy: counterterrorism, conflict resolution, economic development, and good governance. Hence, the U.S. foreign policy makers and implementers must always invoke and implement this new U.S. Foreign Policy by empowering the forces of democratic change and the institutions of good governance in the continent. The mutually beneficial result for the world and humanity will be politically stable and economically strong democratic African states fighting alongside the United States against global terrorism.

The author is a political activist and freelance writer on African diplomatic and political affairs. He can be reached at: kuolpar@ yahoo.com.

CHAPTER FIFTEEN

The High Road to the High-Level Revitalization Forum (HLRF)

The U.S. led and regionally coordinated policy of isolating the largest armed opposition, SPLM/A (IO), since the breakdown of ARCSS beginning on July 8, 2016 triggered a disastrous trajectory of military offensives. Its hallmarks were; a refugee crisis, famine and ethnic cleansing in South Sudan. By all implications, it was a method of giving the existing government a chance to crush the armed rebellion and cow it to the status quo.

That did not happen as the former Obama Administration and the region wanted to see. What embarrassingly transpired was proliferation of armed rebellions throughout the country ushering in new conflicts in regions like Equatoria and Bar El-Ghazal with their own unpredictable dynamics. Kiir's regime found itself in the scalding soup of a political and economic crisis that threatened its very stolen legitimacy. Amidst intense external pressure, they embarked on assorted diversionary tactics.

Those included a national dialogue, the Kampala Initiative for Reunification of the SPLM and so on. In tandem with its strategic allies in the region, the international community was blackmailed and left in the cold without credible and impartial interlocutors to create a genuine political process aimed at ending the crisis.

On the trail to sell these face-saving band-aid initiatives, newly minted terms such as "revitalize" and "estrange" were created to conceal the bloody hands of IGAD in the South Sudanese crisis. The glittering language of this conspiratorial diplomacy was loaded with two fallacious connotations: One was that the opposition parties had deliberately 'estranged' themselves from ARCSS and resorted to violence. This was a malicious portrayal of the armed opposition as the negative force of destabilization in the region.

The other fallacy was that ARCSS was still alive but not inclusively implemented. The salient reason for this reasoning was deliberately omitted.

As a ploy to revive its tarnished reputation and rescue Kiir's regime, the IGAD Head of States Summit held in Addis Ababa, on June 12, 2017 resolved to convene a High-Level Revitalization Forum regarding ARCSS. It was mandated to discuss measures to restore a permanent ceasefire, full implementation of the agreement and to develop a revised and realistic timeline to implement schedules for a democratic election at the end of the interim period.

As stated by Kiir in his address on July 9, 2017 and echoed by Festus Mogea of JMEC, the matrix issued on July 7 outlining the revitalization and subsequent meeting of the IGAD Council of Ministers on July 23/24, for the High Revitalizations Forum was 'not meant for renegotiating ARCSS.'

However, as the consultations with the sponsoring states and the stakeholders progressed, the process took a life of its own. A renegotiation of ARCSS was eventually included. That seriously angered Kiir's regime. The regime responded with a strongly worded statement condemning in what Dr. Martin Lomoro, the regime's Minister of Cabinet Affairs, called it a diplomatic conspiracy against the Republic of South Sudan by certain IGAD member states. Dr. Ismail Wais, the Executive Secretary of IGAD and the Special Envoy was undiplomatically called out in that statement. Even so, the IGAD Secretariat went ahead with their plans to hold Phase I of the HRF.

The Commencement of The High-Level Revitalization Forum

Phase I

Pursuant to the communiqué of the IGAD Head of States and Governments Summit, as endorsed by the sponsoring states, the mandate of the HLRF is threefold:

First to restore a permanent ceasefire. Second to fully and inclusively implement ARCSS. Third to revise the ARCSS implementation schedule in order to hold elections at conclusion of the agreement's timetable.

The IGAD technical team and staff of the JMEC were tasked by IGAD leaders to administer the HLRF. Having recognized that the conflict had evolved since December 2013 with newly emerged movements and the engulfment of the country by the conflict, IGAD and its partners needed to resolve the ambiguities regarding who would participate in the forum and the extent of the agenda.

Without addressing that, the forum could only exacerbate the conflict by further alienating new opposition movements whose grievances were left unaddressed. Hence, IGAD had to determine eligibility and include those estranged groups.

After thorough consultation with all the parties and stakeholders, the HLRF was launched on December 18, 2017 by H.E Haile Mariam Desalegn, Prime Minister of the Federal Democratic Republic of Ethiopia and Chairperson of the IGAD Assembly of Heads of State and Governments, in the presence of H.E Moussa Faki Mahamat, Chairperson of the African Union Commission and H.E Festus Gontebanye Mogae, Chairperson of JMEC.

The forum concluded its first phase with the signing of an Agreement on the Cessation of Hostilities, Protection of Civilians and Humanitarian Access. It was set to come into force at 00:01 (South Sudan local time) on the December 24, 2017.

That set the stage for further discussions, required for the revitalization process. The IGAD Special Envoy for South Sudan, Ambassador Ismail Wais and the Co-Facilitators of the Forum, H.E. Ramtane Lamamra, H.E. Hanna Tetteh and H.E. George Rebelo Chicoti, announced the successful conclusion of the first phase. They expressed their appreciation to the South Sudanese stakeholders, representatives of the government, opposition parties, armed and non-armed groups as well as the representatives of civil society organizations, eminent persons, business, women and youth for the success they achieved. They also congratulated the stakeholders for their commitment in the revitalization process as demonstrated by the constructive manner, in which they participated in the discussions that allowed for the conclusion of an agreement.

The Special Envoy and the co-facilitators called upon the South Sudanese stakeholders to continue with the same spirit in Phase II of the forum. It would deal with issues of governance, a permanent ceasefire, transitional security arrangements and revised timelines for the implementation of ARCSS.

They expressed their gratitude to the envoys and representatives of the partners and organizations for the support and encouragement they rendered to the members of the South Sudanese delegations since their arrival in Addis Ababa. They also spoke on the statements issued by TROIKA, the UN, EU and IPF in support of the forum and urged those organizations and the international community at large to continue accompanying the South Sudanese stakeholders as they forged ahead with the objective of revitalizing and implementing ARCSS.

Phase II - Commenced in Earnest
The second phase was convened on February 05, 2018 in Addis Ababa, Ethiopia.

The forum brought together delegates representing the government, political parties, oppositions, civil society organizations and eminent personalities. High on the agenda was discussing Chapter I and Chapter II of ARCSS without prejudice to the other provisions pertinent to legal and institutional reforms.

Welcoming the participants to the forum, Dr. Workneh Gebeyehu, Ethiopian State Minister of Foreign Affairs and Chairperson of the IGAD Council of Ministers commended the IGAD Member States for their strong commitment in ensuring the successful outcome of the first phase of the revitalization process. The host minister praised the AU, the UN, China, Japan, the Troika, the IPF and all other stakeholders for their unreserved support of the peace process. He highly praised the comprehensive and objective report provided by the JMEC and CTSAMM on the implementation of the Cessation of Hostilities.

Saluting the parties who committed themselves to agreement, Dr. Workneh strongly condemned the violators and spoilers of the truce and stressed that they will be held accountable.

In his opening statement, the Chairperson of the AU, Moussa Faki Mahmat quoted Mahatma Gandhi: "Non-violence is the greatest force at the disposal of mankind. It is mightier than the mightiest weapon of destruction devised by the ingenuity of mankind." Naming the conflict as "a daring insult to the human values," Faki expressed his hope that all the stakeholders to the process would transcend beyond their egos and selfish desires to commit themselves to the ongoing process.

The Deputy Chairperson of JMEC also noted peace is achievable and "What is needed now is a sense of comradeship and the same spirit that was witnessed on the first phase of the HLRF."

Nicholas Haysom, UN special envoy to South Sudan underscored the criticality of inclusivity and called for a comprehensive security arrangement mechanism, strong oversight and monitoring mechanism to fast-track the peace process.

The 10-day long Second Phase Revitalization Process concluded with heads of all parties to the process putting their initials to Chapter I and II of the new ARCSS.

During the closing session, the State Minister for Foreign Affairs of Ethiopia, Hirut Zemene stated, "We have, indeed, made considerable progress, though much remains to be done." Even in areas of disagreement the parties were realistic, transparent and willing to discuss the issues with a view to find common ground. Recalling the breach of the latest CoH, he noted any violations would be subject to punitive measures on the basis of verification reports from CTSAMM.

The forum constructively deliberated on the Declaration of Principles aimed at guiding discussion on the revitalization of the 2015 Peace Agreement. They discussed and agreed on some provisions of Chapter I, and most of the provisions of Chapter II. The agreed articles were initialed by the heads of the delegations. This would ensure that whenever the forum reconvened, it would not revert to deliberation on those provisions.

Ambassador Wais, noted that ongoing bilateral consultations between the various heads of the delegations were very constructive. Although progress was made during Phase II, the gap remained very wide as was evident from the presentations in the plenaries.

Speaking from the experience of previous ARCSS negotiations, I can say with ease and authority that the war-talk attitude has not changed. If anything, it has been compounded by the overwhelming representation of Taban's faction in the government delegation. That group vigorously influenced the government position on power-sharing. Fearing the imminent loss of their share in the next TGoNU, the Crown Hotel groupings were openly demanding an expansion of government to accommodate them. On the other hand, the opposition block presented a totally different proposal for a lean transitional government. Those groups presented a united position for discussing only the principles and structural issues but not power sharing.

The SPLM (IO) Position for HRF

Prior to the commencement of the HRF, the SPLM (IO) unveiled a position paper on the revitalization process of the 2015 peace agreement, demanding a transitional unity government for 27 months. It called for reconstitution of the current transitional unity government, national parliament, cabinet and the judiciary. The SPLM (IO) demanded a reversion to 10 states as per the 2015 peace accord.

In compliance with the ARCSS power-sharing framework, the SPLM (IO) proposed that the selection of the speaker of the traditional legislative assembly, hailing from Equatoria, should be conducted through a democratic process once the expansion of the membership of the assembly was complete.

The SPLM(IO) also proposed dissolution of The Transitional Council of States and its reconstitution with total membership of 50. Five should be from each state of which at least two are female. The SPLM(IO) also emphasized a review of the state constitutions to reflect the devolution of exclusive powers and authorities. Regarding the transitional security arrangement, they demanded that the United Nations Mission in South Sudan and the Regional Protection Force must take over the security of the country for the 18-month transitional period.

Consultation on Outstanding Issues

The consultations to discuss key outstanding issues at the High Revitalization Forum, including positions of the various parties and possible compromises was held in Addis Ababa between February and March 2018.

These were pursuant to the decisions of the IGAD Council of Ministers at its 61st Extraordinary Session on South Sudan that was also held in Addis Ababa on March 26, 2018 to reconvene the continuation of Phase II of the HLRF and to conduct consultations. They would also undertake shuttle diplomacy with the parties and stakeholders to the HLRF to narrow the gaps between the parties prior to the next reconvening of the forum. The consultations focused on the key areas of disagreements on governance and security arrangements re the HLRF.

Under governance, the following issues were discussed:

▌ The composition of the transitional government; structure of the government; responsibility sharing; number of states and the size and composition of the National Legislature.

On security arrangements, the following issues were discussed:

▌ The timeframe for reintegration/unification of forces and an approach to the formation of one national army; security for Juba during the transitional period; demilitarization of civilian centers; cantonment of forces; Security Sector reform and/or the establishment of new security services.

Following extensive deliberations, the representatives of the Civil Society and stakeholders to the HLRF made recommendations for consideration by the parties. Through consultative and proxy approaches, the mediators summarized the following five key areas of sharp disagreements:

1. *On the composition of the Transitional Government:*
   The opposition groups are for the dissolution of the current set up and reconstitution of TGoNU in its current size. The Government is for maintenance of the status quo with limited

expansion to accommodate the so-called estranged groups.

2. *On the structure of the Transitional Government of the National Unity:*
   The opposition alliance excluding the SPLM (IO) proposed a technocratic government or hybrid type without Kiir and Riek. The SPLM (IO) is for the structure provided for in ARCSS but giving the 2nd VP to the Opposition Alliance. The Government is for the maintenance of the current structure but with four Vice Presidents reporting to the President who must be Salva Kiir.

3. *On the number of the states:*
   The opposition groups including the SPLM (IO) demanded reversion back to the ten states as stipulated in ARCSS. The government rejected all that as a non-starter as their (now) 32 states can be altered only through the will of the people during the next constitution.

4. *On the composition of the National Parliament:*
   The government is for expansion of the parliament by 440 members to accommodate so-called estrangement but the all the opposition block including the SPLM (IO) is for a lean legislature with only170 members.

5. *On the Transitional Security Arrangement:*
   The opposition groups were for the demilitarization of all the major towns including Juba as stipulated in Chapter II Article 1 (1.8.1.8, 1.5). The Government has always been against the demilitarization of the major towns. The government has also been opposing the cantonment of forces, this except in what they have called the theatres of the war.

6. *On security sector reforms:*

The opposition groups are for disbarment of the current security sector to be replaced by a new national army. The government is totally opposed to that. They insisted on reforms within the existing structures of the national security sector. Regarding the timeframe for unification of forces, the Government has always demanded immediate unification within the pre-transitional period of 3 months as opposed to the 18 months stipulated in ARCSS.

7. *On the demand of lifting the State of Emergency:*
   The Government rejected that outright as a prerogative of the State under its duty to protect citizens and provide law and order: This is a conventional truth, but the current police state of South Sudan has abused this duty by using it to commit atrocities.

The Workshop

As a way to facilitate deliberations during the HLRF due to start on May 17, 2018, the IGAD mediating team organized a seminar on Governance and Security Arrangements for the key representatives of the parties. It would be leaning on those arrangements to revisit the general principles and practices pertinent to those issues during political transitions. The workshop was held from May15th to refresh and deepen knowledge on subject matters through presentations, case studies, discussions and exercises. The sessions provided participants with key information to enable them to identify optimal security arrangements, power-sharing options and challenges associated with Transitional Government of National Unity.

According to Ambassador Tewolde, IGAD organized the workshop to stimulate insightful discussions and broaden participants' perspectives. The sessions were not for negotiations. The case studies and presentations were meant to enable participants to participate in a non-adversarial environment on the specific challenges of transitioning in the South Sudanese context.

In the joint sessions, the parties were expected to reflect on key lessons straddling governance and security; the linkages between politics and security; guarantees and oversight mechanisms and the gender aspects of governance and security arrangements in a transition.

According to the facilitators, the expected outcomes of the Security and Governance Issues workshop are as follows:

A better understanding of the challenges of the permanent ceasefire and transitional security arrangements.

Common understanding of the key concepts and options for transitional security arrangements.

Enhanced knowledge that enables the participants to think creatively about solutions to the challenges of permanent ceasefire and transitional security arrangements during the HLRF discussions on Chapter II.

Enhanced participants' understanding of the key elements of security processes and key functions of the various implementation institutions and mechanisms.

A better understanding of the possible complementary roles of third parties in the implementation of transitional security arrangements.

The Futile Attempt at Church Mediation

On May 20, 2018, church leaders who were attending the talks as faith-based groups decided to ask the IGAD mediation team to let them moderate the talks as they had better knowledge of the issues.

IGAD granted that in earnest. We could easily see that the government delegation influenced the idea, but we all supported it since the mediation team endorsed it. Justine Badi, the archbishop of the Anglican Church of South Sudan then was elected by the faith-based groups to be the moderator of the process.

The delegations were then broken down into thematic committees, namely a Leadership Committee comprising of the parties' heads of the delegations; a Governance Committee and a Security Committee comprising the technical or support teams of the respective delegations.

As usual, three days of intensive deliberation by the delegations of various participating parties and civil society stakeholders in their respective thematic committees produced no peace. Due to an evident lack of peace-talks experience, the clergy faced difficulties trying to handle the combative behavior of the parties.

For example. In my governance committee, I could not help challenging the moderator. This person tended to forcefully lead us to numerical issues such as counting only which party is assigned take how many positions re power sharing instead of the structural and principle issues of the conflict at hand.

His background in civil engineering was geared more to numbers than to matters of principle. He had no concept regarding how to discuss the substantial issues that justify why some parties deserve more power than others. I could not help pointing out that the subject at hand is not a $1+1 = 2$ situation. It is politics, which is a discipline of argument and debate.

Unfortunately, I hurt his feelings unknowingly. He became furious and said; "I did not expect such tone from our political leaders in this process." Sympathetically, some participants asked me to apologize to him as the only way to ease his nerves. I did so at the opening round of the afternoon session.

As they promised, the church leaders gave it their best, but failed to change the attitude of the warring parties. Prayers and strongly worded sermons could not change the combative attitudes of those who have been arguing since 2014. My friend, Rev. John Jok Chol broke down into tears during the Sunday prayers attended by the parties at Ililly Hotel. To the clergy's dismay, the talks collapsed before them and they were left lamenting with only their prayers for consolation.

In their closing statement, the South Sudan Council of Churches urged the parties to: "Continue their collective search for peace and to cooperate with one another in the spirit of compromise and with IGAD for the sake of the millions of suffering South Sudanese." The three days facilitation of South Sudan Council of Churches was concluded with the signing of Statement of Parties and Stakeholders to recommit themselves to the peaceful settlement of the conflict through the IGAD peace process.

CHAPTER SIXTEEN

Towards the Face-to-Face Phase

After eleven months of intensive engagements and negotiations to revitalize ARCSS as mandated by the IGAD Assembly of Heads of State and Government, on 12 June 2017 ten key Governance and Security issues remained outstanding. The talks then collapsed over those issues.

They were to be found within the two chapters of ARCSS: Power Sharing and the Transitional Security Arrangement.

The whole thing was complicated by the rigid position of the regime. Its negotiating team could only consider the expansion of the government to accommodate the opposition, legitimize their illegitimate regime and maintain the status quo.

As presented by Michael Makuei Lueth in our thematic governance committee, the strategic goal of that position can be summarized as absorption of the SPLA (IO) into their army and accommodation of the political leaders of the opposition in the ministerial portfolios of their government.

In response, we made it abundantly clear that we can not resolve the crisis by affirming the status quo of one man's rule in which the president runs the country without reference to the constitutional institutions. A system without check and balance as a the legislature became rubber stamp of the executive and the judiciary has become just another docket subservient to his office. It was so easy to see why the opposition forces kept directing the debate towards structural and principle related

issues to resolve the conflict and hopefully end it once and for all.
. Unfortunately, the mediators adopted the Government position
and in the new language of the proposed agreement turned the
debate into numerical exercise of positions distribution or responsibility sharing. That mindset ushered in the ever more futile
exercise of presenting flawed proposals, all of which were not
acceptable to the parties. From Addis Ababa to Khartoum and
Kampala, they were produced. The long paper trail included: The
Bridging Proposal of Addis Ababa, The Khartoum Proposal and
the Entebbe Proposals.

The Bridging Proposal

As the parties failed to reach an agreement, IGAD brought forth a
document infamously known as the Bridging Proposal. According
to the mediators, it reflected a considered effort to identify the
middle ground between the respective positions. Unfortunately, it
merely caused the gap to widen.

To the opposition, the bridging proposal was outrageous as it
adopted the position of the Government. It proposed expansion of
the government to accommodate what they referred to as "estranged
groups". Far worse, the draft proposed four vice presidents with the
responsibility to share three ministerial clusters of 42 ministries
each. It also gave Kiir's party the right to appoint the speaker of the
National Assembly (who must hail from Equatoria).

This was alarming to the opposition as it would further empower
Kiir to consolidate his tyrannical grip on the country. The document
further proposed that in the nomination of opposition candidates
for gubernatorial positions in Greater Upper Nile, precedence
should be given to the SPLM/A (IO). In the nomination of opposition candidates for gubernatorial positions in Greater Equatoria,

precedence shall be given to nominations by OPE. The mediators also proposed a six-member High-Level Transition Facilitation Council (TFC) drawn from eminent persons mandated to support the implementation of the agreement.

This was rejected in its entirety by the opposition block and non-partisan stakeholders such as civil societies and the faith-based groups.

The parties and the IGAD mediation team agreed that the revitalization had come to an end. Then they decided to advance the process to three more phases of face to face meetings.

The itinerary of those phases was scheduled as follows:

The first one was to be held in Khartoum on June 25 to discuss the outstanding issues and initial whatever is agreed upon there after which the AU summit will be held.

They would then move to Kenya and continue negotiating the outstanding issues.

Next, they would be off to Addis Ababa for signing.

I wondered out loud what the mediators aimed to achieve with this long itinerary involving all the head of states, some of who are fueling the conflict.

The revitalization initiative was endorsed by IGAD in June 2017, and a new team of special envoys began consultations in August 2017. IGAD Communiqué of the 31st Extra ordinary Summit of IGAD Assembly of Heads of States and Governments on South Sudan, Addis Ababa, June 12, 2017.

On June 23, 2018 the IGAD Mediation Team resolved to end the High Revitalization Forum and gave a two-week deadline from July 21, 2018 for a final deal to be signed in Addis-Ababa.

The First Face-to-Face Encounter

Pursuant to the Resolution of the Extraordinary Meeting of the IGAD Council of Ministers recommending a face-to-face meeting between President Salva Kiir and Dr. Riek Machar before the 31st Summit of the Assembly of the African Union to be held on July 2, 2018 in Noukakchott, Mauritania, the mediation moved the process to the face to face phase. That was to be the first meeting of the two principals under the auspices of Prime Minister Abiy Ahmed on June 21, 2018 with the aim of bridging the gaps between the two warring parties.

Kiir and Machar last met in July 2016 when the crisis erupted at J1 Palace. This encounter produced nothing despite all the threats of the head of states, the AU and TRIOKA during the summit. This was a time when the government position was that of a transition without Riek Machar and the opposition position was for a transition without Salva Kiir.

Kiir told Prime Minister Ahmed "I and Riek Machar can never produce peace even if you keep us for one month in this room". The Prime Minister then washed his hands of the South Sudanese process and asked Machar to go to Khartoum via South Africa. That caused an outcry from the SPLM (IO) as this was seen as him being returned to detention. It also interrupted the ceremony I directed all our Diaspora chapters to launch to celebrate the release of our Chairman.

I had to spend hours on the phone with many leaders of the various chapters. I counseled them to continue celebrating his freedom to also demonstrate the reality on the ground that Dr. Machar has a huge political following. The celebration continued in refugee camps including UNIMISS POCS and throughout the locations of the Diaspora near and far.

To our relief, Dr. Machar was permitted to travel to Sudan via

South Africa and arrived on the following day for the second round of face-to-face talks with Kiir in Khartoum. It then became evident that IGAD had attached Dr. Machar's freedom to negotiating in good faith to bring peace to South Sudan under duress. Upon his arrival in Khartoum, Riek was received and accommodted like a guest of the state but in real life, he was still in the custody of if IGAD. If any thing, one would argue that he was still on parole.

The Khartoum Face-to-Face Phase

In accordance with the Resolution of the 32nd Extraordinary Summit of IGAD on South Sudan, convened in Addis Ababa, Ethiopia, on June 21, 2018, President Omer Hassan Ahmed El-Bashir, the President of the Republic of the Sudan, was authorized to facilitate a second round of face-to-face discussions between H.E. Salva Kiir Miyardit and Dr. Riek Machar Teny to resolve the outstanding issues on governance and security arrangements.

The meeting between the two principals was then held under the auspices of President El-Bashir from the 25th to the 26th of June. The first day of which was graciously attended by H.E. Yoweri Museveni, the President of Uganda.

This second round was concluded with the Khartoum Declaration Agreement. It was then signed and adopted on June 27. It was the road map that eventually led to the signing of the Agreement for a Permanent Ceasefire and Transitional Security Arrangements.

The Khartoum Declaration Agreement stipulated that the permanent ceasefire signed shall be based on the Cessation of Hostilities Agreement signed on December 21, 2017 in Addis Ababa. This agreement stated that within 72 hours of signing, the parties shall agree on all the ceasefire arrangements including disengagement, separation of forces in close proximity, withdrawal of allied troops, opening of humanitarian corridors, and the release of prisoners of war and political detainees. Article 5 of that agreement also stipulated cooperation between Sudan and South Sudan regarding the security of the oil field identified as (Blocks 1, 2, and 4) and Tharjiath (Block 5A) for the resumption and the restoration to previous levels of production.

The Khartoum Power-Sharing Proposal

The Khartoum Mediation team released a revised proposal on July 7, for a power-sharing deal akin to that of the Addis Ababa Bridging Proposal, with some significant variations. Dubbed: The Agreement on Outstanding Issues, it proposed that the incumbent Kiir would continue as the President and Machar, Chairman of the SPLM (IO), would resume his previous position as the First Vice President. The incumbent TGoNU would nominate the second Vice President and other entities would nominate the third Vice President.

The national cabinet was proposed to be 30 members with the following distribution: TGoNU 17, SPLM (IO) 8, SSOA 2, FDs 2 and other parties 1. Nine deputies were proposed and were to be distributed as follows: TGoNU 4, SPLM (IO) 2, FDs 1 and other parties 1. For the national legislature, the document proposed the parliament would consist of 440 members allocated in the following order: TGoNU 266, SPLM (IO) 106, SSOA 46, FD5 5 and other parties 17. That proposal was somewhat acceptable to the SPLM (IO) delegation. We responded and proposed some adjustments on the structure of the presidency, national legislature, state and local governments.

The Entebbe Imposition

The Entebbe power-sharing proposal was the most controversial of all. It adopted the position of the government and even advanced it by giving the TGoNU additional powers to nominate two of the now stated five vice presidents. It expanded the national council of ministers and proposed 45 ministries. For the legislature, it proposed 550 members of parliament.

Worst of all, it included the controversial 32 states (this had increased from the previously unacceptable 28 over time). The opposition block and the civil society stakeholders rejected the entire thing as the most outrageous idea since ARCSS. While presenting it to the SPLM (IO) delegation in Khartoum, the Sudanese Foreign Minister Al-Diridiri Mohamed Ahmed, sounded very threatening. He had this to say: "The SPLM (IO) must understand that they can not get all they want here at the table. They must also understand that no sitting government will negotiate itself out of political power." He went on to say that a good agreement is not one that displaced any members of the government from their current positions.

H.E. Dr. Diridiri made a statement that an agreement has already been reached in Uganda and that the SPLM (IO) must just sign the revised version of the Entebbe Agreement. It became abundantly evident to us that the Khartoum Proposal has been overtaken by Entebbe Proposal. It was solemnly and overwhelmingly rejected by entire opposition block as it diluted the much superior Khartoum version.

This is not the first time President Museveni diverted the process to Entebbe. He tried that in 2015 when the parties were putting the final touches on ARCSS. However, IGAD and the friends of IGAD such as TRIOKA and the EU refused to support him. As such he was forced to join the mediation process in Addis Ababa.

This document was revised many times without significant concessions. After three days of shuttle diplomacy between Khartoum, Kampala and Juba, the final version was presented to us on July 16, 2018.

In his presentation in the plenary attended by all the parties and stakeholders, Ambassador Hammed again tried to blackmail and lie to every party by asserting to each that he had already secured an agreement with the other parties during his consultations.

The proposal Hammad presented to the parties was not any better than before. However, he stated that he had found a middle ground for all parties and announced that the initialing of the document was scheduled for July 17 and set the date for signing ceremony to August 5.

True to his word, Dr. Hammed came back to the parties on July 17 but announced that the mediation has been studying the latest concerns from the parties regarding various provisions in The Agreement on Outstanding Issues. The good news according to him: "There is no outright rejection of the proposal document." The Ambassador then announced to the parties that the initialing of the document was scheduled for July 19 and the signing July 26.

That did not materialize due to the outright rejection by the government citing reservations regarding issues pertaining to power sharing at state and county levels. Not a major surprise as they have been refusing to do so since January 2014.

What boggles minds in this political arrangement is that the party that controls almost two thirds of the countryside is denied control over those same areas. Some of us, myself included, objected to giving the government 55% power in SPLM (IO) controlled areas as per the power-sharing ratios in the central government.

Kiir's regime has an erroneous idea that a bit of political accommodation at the center of government without addressing the fundamental issues such as federalism, institutional reforms and democratization of the political process is adequate to resolve the conflict. It is unfortunate that five years later, he and his cronies are still miss-interpreting the grievances of the opposition as opportunistic political ambition to hold positions in the government.

The Khartoum Peace Agreement on the Outstanding Issues on Governance

Just like ARCSS, the final proposal initialed in Khartoum on August 5, 2018 came at the time when the parties were under intense pressure from the Republic of Sudan to resolve the conflict. It desperately wanted to secure its vital interest regarding South Sudan's oil and the simmering border security issues.

Faced with such vested state interests, the SPLM (IO) risked further diplomatic isolation and possible declaration as a 'negative force'. This was happening at the time when Dr. Machar had just been brought back to the region for the purposes of peace-making.

Kiir was also under the threat of a full U.N. arms embargo and sanctions being imposed despite the progress in the peace process. This final proposal in Khartoum came with both gains and losses for the SPLM (IO). The only significant achievements in this governance and responsibility sharing arrangement is that our Chairman, Dr. Machar would be among the five vice presidents in the new transitionary phase, taking the leadership of the Transitional Council of States. Another achievement was on the Transitional Security Arrangement which provides for cantonment of all the forces, demilitarization of civilian dwelling centers and a merger of forces to create a new army.

On the governance, it goes without informing the records that, the new structures in the presidency and the legislature were imposed by the two foreign presidents (Bashir and Museveni).

Museveni had imposed five vice presidents to accommodate Kiir's two vice presidents and erase the stature of the Executive First Vice President.

All this became very evident when we started discussing the powers allocated to the First Vice President. Those powers ARCSS vested in the First Vice President were to be made shared powers with other four vice presidents. President Museveni's political engineering was very apparent here.

President Bashir imposed the structure of Transitional Legislature. As a result, the 11- page document initialed on July 18, 2015 awarded Juba regime 55% of the political power ratio in state and local governments; SPLM (IO) 27%; to the other political parties 10% and 8% to the rest.

Under this arrangement, the government ministries are as follows: 20 ministers from Kiir's TGoNU, 9 from SPLM (IO) and six from the other groups. The parties also agreed to share the 550-seat parliament with 332 members from Kiir's TGONU, 128 from SPLM (IO) and the balance to the others. All in all, a big gain for Kiir's TGoNU.

Regarding the structure of the presidency, President Kiir would lead the Revitalized Transitional Government of National Unity (RTGoNU) during the transitional period, and Dr. Machar would return to the fold as the First Vice President of South Sudan. That was a gain for both parties. However, as would arise later, Kiir's regime did not want to bring Riek Machar back as the First Vice President with an executive check on the President's powers as stipulated in ARCSS.

Mediators witnessed, the signing of the agreement on governance and responsibility sharing in the Republic of Sudan on August 5, 2018. The agreement signed contained a number of unsettled disputes on some very fundamental issues with regards to the conflict.

The Independent Boundary Commission and the Status of the 32 States

With the issuance of Presidential Order #36 creating 28 states, Kiir did not only violate ARCSS and the Transitional Constitution of South Sudan 2011, but also created permanent conflicts among the indigenous communities regarding the borders.

The only remedy came from IGAD. Pursuant to the decision of 55th Extraordinary Session of the IGAD Council of Ministers held in Addis Ababa, Ethiopia, on January 30-31, 2016, an Inclusive Boundary Commission (IBC) was to be established to determine the number of states and their boundaries in the Republic of South Sudan upon the signing of said Agreement.

The wording of that decision was:

▌ The IBC shall be independent. It shall review the rationale behind the proposal by the SPLM (IO) for the establishment of twenty-one (21) states based on the twenty-one (21) old districts of southern Sudan at the time of Sudan's independence on 01/01/1956. It shall also review the establishment by the government of twenty-eight (28) States created October 2, 2015 that were expanded to thirty-two (32) States on January 14, 2017.

▌ The IBC shall also study the political, security, social and economic viability of the two proposals. They shall ensure boundaries of the states conform to the boundaries of the old districts and provinces of southern Sudan as they stood in January 1, 1956 in order to avoid communal conflicts on land as the land belongs to the community per the Transitional Constitution of the Republic of South Sudan, 2011.

▌ The IBC shall consist of 15 persons: 6 South Sudanese and 9 non-South Sudanese with the necessary skills and knowledge to undertake its functions. Among the 6 South Sudanese at least 2 shall be women. The 9 non-South Sudanese shall be as follows: 3 from IGAD, 3 from the AU Ad-hoc High-Level Committee (C5) and 3 from Troika. The parties: 2 from the Government, 2 from SPLM (IO), 1 from SSOA and 1 from OPP, shall nominate the South Sudanese.

- The IBC shall be chaired by a non-South Sudanese and may obtain the services of a team of experts.
- The IBC shall complete its work before the commencement of the Transitional Period and within 180 days and shall make recommendations. Thereafter it shall be dissolved.
- To enhance its efficiency, the IBC shall establish 3 teams, each consisting of 5 representatives and relevant experts, to be deployed at locations it will designate.
- If the work of the IBC is not conclusive within the period mentioned above, the country shall revert to 10 states according to ARCSS 2015.
- The IBC shall submit its findings and recommendations to IGAD, NCAC and the parties before the commencement of the Transitional Period for implementation and incorporation into the agreement.

Discussion on the Bracketed Provisions of Khartoum Peace Agreement (KPA)

The Khartoum Peace Agreement was signed with several bracketed issues but on a positive note that the way forward would be decided in another IGAD Council of Ministers meeting.

That meeting transpired as 64th Extraordinary Session of the IGAD Council of Ministers held in Khartoum on August 9 and10, 2018 to discuss issues and to prepare the full document of a Comprehensive Revitalized ARCSS.

The opening session was attended by the partners including the AU, UN, EU, IPF, China and TRIOKA. Chaired by H.E. Hirut Zemene, State Minister of Foreign Affairs of the Federal Democratic Republic of Ethiopia, they adopted an implementation matrix and resolved that the Khartoum round of talks would continue until August 19. The meeting resumed on the 11th with a briefing regarding how to go about discussing the bracketed articles. The agenda was distributed for deliberation. The items to discuss were:

1   Article 4: Number of states and IBC issues.
2   Roles and functions of the Presidency.
3   Judicial Reforms.
4   Composition of the National Constitutional Amendment Committee (NCAC).
5   Creation of five ministries and their clustering.

While deliberating on the above, the parties discovered that there were no real agreements within the Khartoum Peace Agreement on the resolution of the bracketed articles which were critically fundamental in order to reach a substantial agreement towards the resolution of the conflict.

As mentioned previously, there could be no real and implementable agreement without addressing the roles and functions of the president and the vice presidents, state boundaries, constitutional amendments and judicial reforms.

To complete the revitalization of ARCSS, its substantial provisions needed to be reviewed, updated and amended if necessary. Among those are the amendments from Chapters 3 to 8 of the agreement that cover humanitarian assistance and reconstruction, economic and financial management, transitional justice and reconciliation.

The others are regarding the parameters of a permanent constitution, a joint monitoring and evaluation commission, supremacy of the agreement and procedures for amendments to it.

Hence, for those of us who negotiated it, we signed an agreement that was not actually an agreement at all.

As mentioned in prior pages, the whole thing was bulldozed by Ambassador Diridiiri Ahmed, the Chief Mediator who held that the document must be signed regardless. This merely created a false and misleading inference that an actual agreement had been signed.

In any case, the historic agreement signed in Khartoum on the 5th of August 2015 was neither historic nor an agreement. This would come back to haunt the parties on August 16, 2018 when we relapsed back to the war-talking attitude.

For example; regarding the powers, functions and responsibilities of the first vice president and the other vice presidents; Michael Makuei Lueth uttered that with existence of the new four vice presidents, the first vice president loses those executive powers conferred upon him by ARCSS. Under the new agreement, he will now share them on consultative basis with the other vice presidents and the president.

Those powers are the ones stipulated in Article 6 (6.1, 6.3.1, 6.3.3.8 & 6.3.9). They pertain to the first vice president's responsibility to ensure that the agreement and the reforms ARCSS brings to the government are implemented. A sub-section of Article 6 (6.3.1) explicitly stipulated that the first vice president shall coordinate the implementation of the agreement and initiate institutional reforms as provided for in ARCSS. Article 6 (6.3,9) substantiates that provision by stipulating that the first vice president shall follow up and ensure the implementation of the Council of Ministers' decision with relevant ministries and institutions.

In contrast with his previous functions and powers to chair

all government independence meetings, the first vice president is responsible for chairing only the Governance Cluster of the Council of Ministers in the new set up under the Khartoum Peace Agreement. That includes the independent commissions under the governance cluster.

That pitted my committee No.3 regarding the Function and Roles of the Presidency against that of our counterpart in the Government Delegation under the leadership of Michael Makuei Lueth who was accompanied by Ambassador Mayen Dut.

After extensive discussions on those powers, the SSOA and the other parties sided with TGoNU delegation to advance that there is nothing special about the role that should allow him to be the custodian of a Revitalized ARCISS implementation. Our counter-argument was based on the premise that Article 1.3 and 1.4 of Khartoum Peace Agreement as stipulated in ARCSS reaffirmed the seniority of our First Vice President.

The mediators aligned with the others to shut us down. We stood our ground and maintained that we do not want to see even a punctuation mark on our powers and functions on the document.

I concluded my presentation by reminding the mediators that scrapping our powers would cause disagreements that would undermine the spirit of Khartoum Peace Agreement.

Using the mood against our position in the room, Ambassador Mayen Dut from the background stated that: "your Chairman could find himself in South Africa and can negotiate with us there if you insist on acquiring those powers." He said this while I was still making my presentation on those issues. I overheard his utterance, but I was too occupied with the presentation to clearly understand it. Fortunately, my colleague Puot Kang jotted it down for me. We then moved out and drafted a letter of protest dated August 15, 2018 addressed to the Special Envoy. It read:

HE. Amb. Dr. Ismail Wais

Special Envoy on South Sudan peace talks.

Subject: Protest Against Ambassador Mayan Dut's Threatening Statement.

Your Excellency,

In reference to the above subject, we the SPLM/ (IO) delegation in the Committee Number 3 to discuss power sharing at the Presidency level submit this letter to Your Excellency to protest today's threatening statement by Ambassador Mayen Dut of South Sudan that the Chairman of SPLM (IO), Dr. Reik Machar Teny will be taken back to South Africa to negotiate with us in that country if he does not concede the powers he is still claiming those under Article (3.1, 3.3.1, 3.3.8 and 3.3.10).

Your Excellency, this intimidating utterance violates the spirit of what we have so far achieved here in Khartoum. With the apparent failure of the mediators to rebuke Ambassador Dut to withdraw his undiplomatic statement, we have been made to conclude that such a pronouncement by a senior diplomatic representative accredited to this country is based on the informed position of the government to get its way through intimidating the SPLM (IO) in these talks. This is not a conducive spirit in which to continue negotiating with the government delegation without withdrawing that statement. Hence, we have decided to withdraw from that committee to discuss the issues under discussion until we receive a formal statement to withdraw that statement.

We sincerely appreciate your effort to bridge the gap between the parties to resolve the ongoing conflict in our country through peaceful means. We look forward to hearing from the other party through your good offices soon.

Thank You,

Stephen Par Kuol

Head of the SPLM-IO Team to Committee Number 3.

In response to that protest letter, the IGAD mediators invited us to a plenary attended by the TGoNU, SSOA and the Other Parties (OPP). Comrade Puot and I attended that meeting on August 15, 2018 to hear from them as I requested.

The Chair of the meeting, Ambassador Frey of Ethiopia then asked the SPLM (IO) to speak first. I then took the floor and presented my protest letter and demanded apology from the TGoNU if we were to proceed with the deliberations. Makuei then took the floor and apologized on behalf of the TGoNU delegation but said Stephen and the SPLM (IO) should not make a big deal out of this because we have often joked about more serious things than that. The Chair then asked me to accept that apology on behalf of the SPLM (IO). That I did but stressed that we can joke about everything else but not about South Africa!

I went on to bring to their attention that IGAD was on record acknowledging that it was responsible for Riek Machar's detention in South Africa. So, an utterance by the accredited Ambassador of South Sudan to Sudan, which is now leading the process, cannot be taken lightly. Although South Sudan is a warring party in this process, it is also diplomatically recognized as a member of IGAD, which is leading this process. Thus, its official statement by a senior diplomatic representative like Ambassador Mayen Dut should not be taken as a casual joke. Dr. Ismail Wais then apologized on behalf of IGAD and we moved on with negotiations. I then presented the SPLM (IO) position as follows:

SPLM/IO Negotiation Team on the Presidency
15th August 2018

HE. Amb. Dr. Diridiri Momhed Ahmed,
IGAD Chief Mediator for South Sudan Peace Talks
Khartoum, Sudan

Re- the SPLM (IO) Position on the Functions of the First Vice President.

Your Excellency,

As we have made very clear during the committee deliberations from August 14 to 15, 2018, scrapping the functions of the First Vice President by sharing them with other vice presidents is a violation of Article (1.3). Read together with Article (1.4) of the Khartoum Peace Agreement on the Outstanding Issues of Governance, the agreement recognizes Dr. Riek Machar Teny as the First Vice President with higher political status than the other four vice presidents. Pursuant to such provisions, we have resolved to retain those functions and will not initial any draft that tampers with them as stipulated under the provisions of ARCSS as follows:

First Vice President of the Republic of South Sudan:

1.1   For the duration of the Transition, there shall continue to be the office of the First Vice President of the Republic of South Sudan, to supervise the implementation of the reforms outlined in this Agreement and exercise the powers, functions and responsibilities outlined below. The office of the First Vice President shall cease to exist at the conclusion of the Transition Period unless other-wise decided in the permanent Constitution;

1.2   The Chairman of the SPLM/A-IO Dr. Riek Machar Teny shall assume the position of the First Vice President of the Republic of South Sudan for the duration of the Transitional Period;

1.3   The Powers, Functions and Responsibilities of the First Vice President shall be to:

1.3.1   Coordinate the implementation of this Agreement

and initiate institutional reforms as prescribed in this
Agreement;

1.3.2   Serve as Commander-in-Chief of the SPLA-IO during
the Pre-Transitional Period and until the unification of
forces;

1.3.3   Serve as the Acting Commander-in-Chief of the unified
Armed Forces in the event of any temporary absence of
the President after the unification of the forces;

1.3.4   Chair and oversee the Governance Cluster.

1.3.5   Serve as Deputy Chair of EFMA Board.

1.3.6   Serve as Deputy Chair of the NSC.

1.3.7   Serve as Deputy Chair of the NDC.

1.3.8   Oversee the preparation and consideration of Revitalized
TGoNU business and programs.

1.3.9   Follow up and ensure the implementation of the Council
of Ministers' decisions with the relevant Ministries and
institutions within the Governance Cluster; see implementation of laws passed by the Transition.

1.3.10 Carry out other functions as may be prescribed by law,
as long as such laws do not contradict the terms of this
Agreement as stipulated in this Agreement.

Thank You,

Stephen Par Kuol
Head of the SPLM-IO team to Committee Number 3 on
Governance and Responsibilities Sharing.

I registered the negotiating position of SPLM (IO) on those provisions. I told them that they could not change even a comma, or
any other punctuation mark to tamper with the threads of meaning
within those articles.

Unfortunately, as the mediators indicated during deliberations, they bought Michael Makuei's polemical insistence that there is nothing so special about Riek Machar for him to be granted executive powers that other vice presidents do not enjoy during the transitional period. As such, they brought forth the final draft without the functions and powers of the first vice president as stipulated in ARCSS.

This became a setback to the process as we refused to initial the agreement without those provisions. With this, the TGoNU team had the last laugh as they made gains both in the governance and security arrangements that they had been pushing since the Addis Ababa phases. The talks were then adjourned for seven days for the hosts to celebrate the Muslim Enid Zeya El Mubarak. Intense consultation with the Government of Sudan was to follow.

Hiccups On the Bracketed Outstanding Issues

As scheduled, the talks resumed on the 25th of August and the parties started deliberating on the bracketed issues of Chapter I (Governance) and Chapter II (Security Arrangements), along with Chapters III-VIII that were not discussed before. It was hoped that this would revitalize ARCSS. The parties had been served on the 20th with a draft text for observation and notation. The Mediation Committee then scheduled the initialing of the final draft for the 27th at 4PM.

Unfortunately, parties could not agree on the following four outstanding critical issues:

The decision-making threshold. The decision-making mechanisms and quorums did not take into consideration the new increase in numbers at the Executive level, the Council of Ministers and the

Legislature. In ARCSS, we had only two vice presidents. In this R-ARCSS, we have became five.

Simply put, Kiir would need only one of the vice presidents from the other parties to run their program through without the principle of collegial decision-making. The Council of Ministers was 23 in ARCSS when the Cabinet was 33. The government side now insisted on 41 Ministers of which they have 23. Thereby they alone could hold a quorate meeting of the Council of Ministers and pass resolutions or even amend this agreement.

The Permanent Constitutional Making Process.

The parties could not agree on procedures for this. The opposition maintained that constitution making is conventionally a people-driven process that does not only need wider consultation with all the segments of the society but must also be backed by the voices and aspirations of the people in the National Constitutional Conference as provided for in ARCSS. Taking a contrary position, the government is for a state-controlled process using the existing Constitutional Review Commission to prepare the draft Constitutional Bill for deliberation in the National Constitutional Conference.

In the presentation I made, I brought it to the attention of the mediators and observers that South Sudan has a tragic history of constitution making which is responsible for the ongoing conflict. Juba is addicted to dictating things to the people including social contracts such as a constitution. That is why we demand that our people must be given an opportunity to break that cycle by according them the space to write their own constitution.

Deployment of Ugandan and Sudanese troops as peace-keepers to enforce implementation.

The Agreement on Security Arrangements signed in Khartoum on the 6th of July stipulated that Sudan and Uganda were the guarantors of the Agreement. However, the semi-final draft failed to provide mechanisms to enable those guarantors to contribute to the peacekeeping mission in South Sudan to enhance protection and security throughout the implementation of the Agreement.

Regarding the Transitional Security Arrangement, the SPLM (IO) and SSOA demanded that the deployment of the forces by the guarantors must include Kenya and Ethiopia. The parties also demanded that the forces be deployed to operate within the mandate of the United Nations Mission in South Sudan including training the unified forces and monitoring the Permanent Ceasefire through established mechanisms such as RPF and the aforesaid UNMISS.

The Disagreement on the TBC and IBC.

The IGAD Assembly of Heads of State and Government held in Khartoum on the 5th of August had decided that Article 4 and 4a re the number and boundaries of States in the Agreement on Governance signed on the 5th of August be opened-up for renegotiation. That was done on the 13th.

Following that the mediators prepared a text reflecting the consensus reached in those discussions. It appeared as Annex D in the draft that was presented to the parties on the 20th.

Having found themselves under pressure and threats by the government delegation saying they were not signing any agreement that included Annex D, the Mediators removed it.

There was an abhorrent reaction from the SPLM (IO) and SSOA when the mediators declared that this was a final text of the agreement and that the parties were invited to sign it on the 28th of August 2018. The two groups objected to a referendum set by the mediation as the default solution to fix the disagreement over the 32 states unilaterally established by President Kiir.

So, first they make the call to re-establish the old 10 states as the default option. Then, they initiate a referendum as the default option but added two new elements. The first was to review the current boundaries of the states and to ensure their conformity to the 1.1.1956 tribal border. The second option is that the people would be asked if they want the 10 states system or the 32-state regime.

Over this dispute, the SPLM (IO) and SSOA declined to initial the agreement. The plenary was held on the morning of August 28, 2018 at 10AM. As per usual, H.E. Dr. Diridiri Hammed, the Chief Mediator announced that the parties, with the exception of the SSOA, agreed to initial the document now.

Being the head of the SPLM (IO) four plus one delegation in the plenary, I could not allow that to go without objection. I raised my hand to register our position for the benefit of the audience. The Chief Mediator gave me the floor and I shocked everyone by announcing that the SPLM (IO) would not initial the agreement until the outstanding issues are all resolved.

Dr. Diridiri could not believe his ears. He had to ask me to repeat what I said. I rose again and made it abundantly clear that the SPLM (IO) was not ready to initial the document citing the four outstanding issues mentioned afore. That silenced the room and closed the session for the day. Dr. Diridiri then declared that the process is over and initialing is optional. Take it or leave it!

The TGoNU and FDs then initialed the document. Addressing the press at the doorstep, Dr. Diridiri announced to the press that the SPLM (IO) and SSOA have declined to initial but the document would go the IGAD Head of States in any event. It became evident that the agreement could only be complete once those two major groups came aboard.

In fact, it caused a sort of fever amongst the stakeholders and the mediators. The consultation continued between the two parties (IO and SSOA). They resolved to seek an audience with President

Omar Bashir. He granted it and invited Dr. Machar to see him that same evening.

During the meeting, Machar presented the four points including the decision-making mechanism. President Bashir responded positively and promised that he would convene an extraordinary summit of the IGAD Head of States and present those points prior to the summit in which the agreement was to be approved for final signature.

Based on that promise, the SPLM (IO) and SSOA met and decided to initial the agreement with reservations attached for tabling at the forthcoming IGAD extraordinary summit in Khartoum.

The two groups agreed to submit separate position papers to the mediators. However, I also recommended that we issue joint press statements to explain our position to the media and to the South Sudanese public. They had the right to know why we reconsidered initialing the document. That was seconded by Dr. Lam Akol and the Honorable Gabriel Changson of the SSOA. It was then approved by the Chairman Dr. Riek Machar. My colleague, Josephine Joseph Lagu and I were then assigned to draft it as follows:

Joint Press Statement by The SPLM and SSOA

The Sudan People's Liberation Movement SPLM (IO) and the South Sudan Opposition Alliance (SSOA) issue this joint press statement to inform the people of South Sudan, the Mediation, the International Community and friends of South Sudan Worldwide that after intensive and lengthy consultation with the mediation and His Excellency President Omar Al Bashir, President of the Republic of Sudan, the host of this peace process, we have decided to initial the draft of the Revitalized Agreement on the Resolution of the Conflict in South Sudan (R-ARCSS). However, we want to make it abundantly clear to the public that this initialing is conditional upon the assurance that the four concerns raised on Tuesday 28/8/2018 be tabled for discussion by President Al Bashir in the forthcoming 64th Extraordinary summit of the IGAD head of States and governments as promised in those meetings. In summary, the critical concerns raised are as follows:

The decision-making mechanism in the Presidency, Legislature, Council of Ministers and the state and local govern-ments must be adjusted to protect the agreement by ensuring that one party does not use the tyranny of majority to amend the agreement at will, without agreement from the other parties. We therefore recommend three quarters or higher instead of two-thirds or simple majority to make any decision.

Re the dispute on determining the number of states and demar-cation of the tribal and state boundaries. We, the parties issuing this statement demand that in the event that the Referendum Commission on the Number of States and Boundaries (RCNSB) fails to carry out the referendum on time, IGAD Heads of State and Government recommend the appropriate number of states and the boundaries to establish the Revitalized TGoNU. Along this line, we demand that ARCSS incorporate Annex D into the body of the final Agreement as stipulated in articles 4 and 4a of the Revitalization Agreement on the Conflict Resolution in South Sudan (R-ARCSS)

The procedures of the permanent constitutional-making process. In compliance with conventional best practices, we demand that the Permanent Constitutional Making Process must be people driven. We are stressing this point, in objection to the government control method presented by the incumbent TGoNU.

On the Transitional Security Arrangement. We propose that instead of Uganda and Sudan alone, the deployment of the forces by the guarantors includes Kenya and Ethiopia and that the forces are deployed to operate within the mandate of the United Nations Mission in South Sudan (UNMISS). We also recommend their mandate to include the training of the unified forces and monitoring the Permanent Ceasefire through established mechanisms such as RPF and UNMISS.

Finally, the SPLM/A-IO and SSOA concluded by urging the mediation to resolve these critical matters of contention for us to sign the final text of the R-ARCSS.

We remain seized to reach a final sustainable peace agreement as soon as possible.

Khartoum, Sudan (August 30, 2018).

CHAPTER SEVENTEEN

The Images of the War Talks

" *Conflict is not all bad. Its existence is the only guarantee that aspiration of society will be attained.*
                                                         John Burton 1972

Conflict arises from differences, both large and small. It occurs whenever people disagree over their values, motivations, perceptions, ideas, or desires. Sometimes these differences appear trivial, but when a conflict triggers strong feelings, it can be personally internalized. Conflict begins in the mind and that is where it must be ended. In other words, conflict ends when it ends in the mind of the men who initiated it.

Hence, conflict resolution must be correctly conceived as a mental exercise to address the grievances that triggered it in the minds of the parties concerned. As we have seen during the course of the raging civil war in South Sudan, resolving a conflict while it is still raging in people's minds without addressing the underlying grievances that triggered it is a futile exercise.

From the experiences of the Arusha Intra-SPLM Dialogue to the ARCSS negotiation and the High Revitalization Forum (HRF), we have witnessed that peace talks and agreements do not end conflicts.

Over the five years of the war and peace process, cessation of hostility and permanent ceasefire agreements were signed but the hostilities continued to rage. It was all due to the fact that the conflict was and is still raging in the minds of the warring parties.

This lengthy experience has demonstrated that there can never be partners in peace without genuine peace of mind. Without this mindset for peace, you can only have warring parties masquerading as peace partners. Speaking from the five years experience of this peace process, none of the parties wanted to skip any sessions, but there were no 'peace-talks' at the peace-talks. It has been always been a public relations exercise for the most part. As such, peacemaking was given lip service at the peace table in forigen lands but the mindset was war-making on the ground in South Sudan.

As some of the following images clearly exhibit, the South Sudanese conflict is psychologically internalized and highly personalized. That cannot be more telling than in these pictures I have called images of the war-talks. However, a photograph can't capture people's voices or convey what is lingering in their minds. Even written presentations might not tell you much. What people say often doesn't accurately reflect what they are actually thinking and feeling. That 'can' be clearly captured in photos and videos. The physical nuances of the actors in question are on full display.

In fact, people sometimes use verbalizations to modify, filter, and censor the expression of what goes on inside their minds. Scientific research in psychology has empirically concluded that non-verbal communication reveals as much, or more, than verbal. This is because much of what happens with body language is unconscious and spontaneous. People can monitor and control it to a certain degree, but often their physical bearing conveys their feelings when they aren't verbalizing them, even when they don't want to.

In this case, the physical interactions as dictated by diplomacy in those peace talks can be deceptive. However, the body doesn't know how to lie. Body language in a photograph never occurs in a vacuum. The photo conveys the truth of what is in the mind of the subject. The way our leaders interact in public speaks volumes of the cold truth that reconciliation is a far-fetched concept as things stand today in South Sudan.

Among the photos, the warring state of mind is clearly captured in that first face to face encounter between the two principals in Addis Ababa, the Entebbe meeting and others. These range from the 2015 interactions in Addis Ababa to those including the verbal confrontation between President Uhuru Kenyatta and Salva Kiir where Kenyatta was angrily pressuring him to sign ARCSS in July 2015.

In those pictures, the image of rage is sharp and loud in the face of the man we expect to lead the nation to peace and reconciliation. The face and hands play a critical role in expressing emotion and exposing the mental state. Biologically, these areas of the body are rich in nerve endings. Disproportionately large areas of the brain are devoted to processing information about what's happening there. This attests to the scientific fact that it is not what you say but how well that rhymes with your body language.

This was clearly captured on camera during the interaction between the principals in the Entebbe Palace of President Yowery Museveni. It is clearly evident that wearing a diplomatic face during a raging conflict is humanly difficult.

The only person I have seen composed in his interaction with his political enemies is Dr. Machar. The way he courageously and courteously approached IGAD and Kiir after they had illegally detained him in South Africa for two years speaks volumes regarding the temperament of the man as a leader.

Most flagrant of all was the snub he received from Kiir in his attempt to reach out to him upon signing the agreement on power sharing and governance in Khartoum on the August 5, 2015. Dr. Machar did not stop there. Again, he reached out to Kiir between the podium and the seating area with a huge hug and broad smile. Kiir did not have any choice but to reply in kind towards a man he hates to death.

Salva Kiir then tried his level best to observe diplomatic etiquettes in Khartoum but relapsed back to his spontaneous state of mind upon his arrival at Juba International Airport on August 6, 2018 where he blasted Dr. Machar for intransigence and violations of the Cessation of Hostility Agreements.

Those who know the man would tell you that Salva Kiir is not working for peace but for war. That is the only way to prolong his illegitimate rule of guns and violence. With his public pronouncements and blatant violation of all agreements, Kiir has proven beyond a reasonable doubt that he fears peace more than war and will never gather the courage to face this conflict as a leader.

Conflict resolution requires steadfast courage and much consideration. Fearing a conflict that is already consuming society is not an option. It must be faced head on. Conflict resolution needs a collaborative exercise that involves listening to each other to identify areas of agreement and ensuring that all parties understand each other as fully as possible. In other words, the parties must make each other feel safe, secure, respected, trusted and valued. This means a discourse without strong emotions but with cold analytical minds using critical thinking. This is required to address underlying grievances and to defuse unfounded or wrongly perceived fears.

Peacemaking must be first and foremost conceptualized as a long process, not an event. It demands genuine soul searching and trust building over time. All those factors are sadly missing in the South Sudanese peace process. That is why I call it war talk.

John Burton, one of the most renowned academic authorities in the field of conflict resolution, observed that conflict is not all bad as it is an essential element in human relationships "It is a means to a change. In other words, it is a means by which our social values of welfare, security, justice, and opportunities for community development can be achieved." A society without conflict does not exist and imagining something like that is utopian at best.

Thus, it must be faced as a reality to be addressed and managed principally and structurally. Unfortunately, the government of the day in Juba has internalized the erroneous notion that the opposition parties have taken arms or turned violent to gain positions in the government. This shuns debate on the issues behind the conflict and reduces the grievances of the opposition to 'job search through political violence'. This has bred nothing but mutual mistrust. So far it has eluded any meeting of minds gathered to resolve the conflict. Every party has then stuck to its guns in its own trench. The parties then resigned to animosity without any genuine attempt to face the problem.

The old chicken and egg question is: "Should it be dialogue or reconciliation first?" Of course, the conventional practice is to use dialogue as a means to attain reconciliation. That would be the ultimate goal. Yet, reconciliation can come only when grievances are recognized and discussed for resolution.

Unfortunately, there is overriding judgmental mentality embracing political violence beyond reason in South Sudan at the time of this writing. This vicious mentality of war as an end in itself thwarts strategic thinking and the culture of reconciliation through dialogue.

The decay of that culture of political violence is amply demonstrated by the shameful fact that dialogues are externally initiated and imposed upon us to address foreign interests. Speaking from the ARCSS experience, we witnessed that imposed dialogue can only produce-imposed agreements that can be violated with impunity. That has resulted in sharply eroded confidence between the warring parties.

With the return to war in July 2016, the continuous violation of the COH and President Kiir's verbal and body language that still communicates only war, conflict and violence is currently established as the norm. It is ingrained into the collective psyche of the people of South Sudan that the warring parties can never bring peace to South Sudan. This was confirmed by Salva Kiir's presentation at the Juba International Airport on August 6, 2018 in which told the people of his reservations that led to the breakdown of ARCSS and killed any hope for a speedy resolution.

The First encounter since December 2013 where Bishop Deng Bul (in red), is praying with President Kiir and Dr Riek Machar in Addis Ababa, Ethiopia. He expected to reunite the adversaries through higher being.

President Omar Al-Bashir, in one-on-one hard talks with Salva
Kiir. As usual, Kiir appears too defensive to take responsibility for
war and peace in South Sudan.

Forced handshakes and tense angry gazes. A mockery of the
mediation of Museveni. This is a true image of the war talks.
Clearly, one can conclude that Salva Kiir is being coerced by
Museveni to shake hands with Dr Machar.

President Uhuru Kenyatta's hand gesture depicts harsh diplomacy with President Salva Kiir when he refused to sign ARCSS as he promised earlier. His cronies look very upset.

Rebecca Garang broke down hysterically when Kiir refused to sign ARCSS in Addis Ababa. It was an agreement that would to bring to an end the suffering of the South Sudanese women and children. Two ladies of the Women's Block had to jump in to comfort her.

President Salva Kiir snubbing Dr Machar's extended hand during the signing ceremony. Kiir and his cronies said he was busy and did not see him. However, it was embarrassing to all present.

In this image, Salva Kiir appears hyper-vigilant and irritable with Dr Lam Akol for greeting President Omar El Bashir before greeting him. Honorable Awut Deng, the lady in blue behind President Kiir, was also resentful and accused Dr Lam of deliberately ignoring the President during the first face-to-face meeting in Addis-Ababa.

CHAPTER EIGHTEEN

Lessons Learned

One of the most important lessons we learned in this experience of peace making in South Sudan is that the durability of peace agreements usually depends on the extent to which the key parties to the conflict take genuine ownership of it by making themselves protagonists, not antagonists.

We have also learned that agreements do not automatically deliver peace where the protagonists have a long history of engaging in confrontational politics like in South Sudan. The SPLM/A culture of political militarism often produces nothing but agreements that are fraught with tension, suspicion and mistrust. As witnessed during the CPA, these factors always resulted in selective implementation of the agreement and violation of certain provisions. Such actions often lead to a resurgence of conflict.

That is exactly what we witnessed in July 2016. In truth, there was no peace mindset. We were just engaging in zero-sum games for the purposes of shifting the balance of power within in our conflicting cocoons. Experiences elsewhere have proven that conclusive and through implementation of peace agreements usually depends on the political will of the parties to the agreement. This was clearly missing in ARCS where President Salva Kiir signed the agreement without agreeing with its content.

According to Professor Rudolph Rummel: "The imposition of deadlines to force warring parties to sign agreements even in circumstances when the end justifies the means succeeds in getting signatures on papers but largely fails to secure the much-needed peace, as parties are usually reluctant and unwilling to implement actions." He also points out that the making of peace is with the aim of achieving a balance of power. This requires an interlocking of mutual interests, capabilities and wills. Negotiating peace agreements requires patience, persistence and determination.

The IGAD mediators should have engaged with all the parties to any proposed agreement and dialogue on the reservations and red lines of either side. That way, the players either come to outright disagreement or enter into a true and implementable agreement. It was not the case for ARCSS. The agreement was imposed without a coordinated enforcement mechanism. Tragically, the experience of ARCSS caused loss of confidence in the mediators and among the parties. This has not been resolved to date.

Another delicate lesson learned from the ARCSS negotiations is the ugly truth that the mediation was suffering from credibility crisis. One of the most gross tragedies of the conflict in South Sudan is that the process to resolve it is led by regional states that have been deeply involved in fueling the crisis from day one The media- tors are both judges and the defendants in the court of war and peace. Some countries that directly or indirectly involved in the fighting are also members of IGAD, which also use their club membership to make decisions slanted to benefit themselves. Out of seven countries, three are parties to the war. Those are Uganda, South Sudan and Kenya. Despite the obvious, even Kenya and Uganda masquerade as part of a united front to mediate the warring parties. In defiant of all international diplomatic and humanitarian standards, Kenya has taken sides in the conflict and facilitated state terrorism by Juba in its own capital Nairobi where key members of the opposition and civil rights activists were kidnapped and illegally deported to Juba. Djibouti and Somalia are reluctant bystanders.

In addition to self-serving members, IGAD does not seem to have any vision for peace in South Sudan. Any initiatives they have brought to the table have not been supported by any long-term, consistent strategy required to successfully implement it.

If there is such a strategy, it is not rooted in objective under-standing of the conflict, interests and positions sustaining the situation in South Sudan. IGAD is not just an ineffectual mediator by design, it is so by default. Its record in the then Sudan and Somalia are testimonials to ineptitude. History has shown that IGAD is hapless and could never actually broker a peace deal until the parties were either in a stalemate that was malignant to both, or one party was weakened to the extent that any compromise was a good outcome.

In most cases, IGAD simply watches a conflict unfold and then go into high gear by rolling out such shopworn clichés as; 'noted with concern', 'regretted', 'underlined its resolve' and 'condemned the escalating fighting by the parties'. Better yet they love to call upon the parties to participate in endless forums, fact-finding missions and meetings. The recent long itinerary of talks that circled the region from Addis Ababa, to Khartoum, to Nairobi tells us that IGAD mediation is all about holding numerous meetings & publicity events. They make recommendations and hurl overheated threats to force peace but never follow up to make these things happen. I refer to it as hot air diplomacy. Maybe better to simply call it hot air.

As we have experienced from January 2014 onwards, the deciding factor for IGAD diplomacy has always been the military strength of the parties on the ground. The stronger party gets favorable treatment. Period.

Conversely, irrespective of the strength and the logic of the weaker party's negotiating positions, IGAD will simply ignore them and recklessly bulldoze its way to the finish line.

That is precisely what it has just done in Khartoum by imposing an agreement that favors the party with mightier firepower but one without a national political agenda. Ultimately, we have learned beyond any reasonable doubt the fallacy behind the 'African problem, African solution' theory. This method has been exhausted in the case of the South Sudanese crisis. IGAD mediation has failed miserably.

In my humble view, the only durable solution will come only through decisive policy direction of one or more of the United Nations 'big five' (US, Russia, China, UK and France) at the UNSC in New York.

Otherwise, our experience has shown that IGAD is a servant of those with big guns or money. Only a promise to spend bucketloads of dollars on IGAD's many meetings and cascading communiqués will get IGAD running into (fruitless) action.

The big five have the power to intervene by using diplomatic leverage (and more) on the key regional players. Essentially, they can bring pressure to bear on those countries to find a real, fair and lasting solution. Only those global powers can advise the regional states that investing in Kiir's tyranny is not in the best interest of their country and will bring severe hardship to them if they continue.

The technical credentials of the mediation team of special envoys was another shortcoming. Although Ambassador Seyoum Mesfin, the Chief Mediator gave it his best, a true mediator must have vision, a strategy and a principled commitment to peace-making. IGAD does not have even one person that fits the bill! A true mediator cannot publicly say there is no military solution while its actions show that peace can only be brought by military might.

A mediator occupies a fiduciary position and acts gain public the public trust. The question that has been buzzing in so heads is: What on earth is IGAD doing in the business of peace making in South Sudan? How do people still expect IGAD to embark on a credible and inclusive revitalization of the peace process when that is fundamentally and irreparably incompatible with the character and interests of IGAD members both individually and collectively? The multiple forums endlessly sprung up by individual IGAD members is a pretty good indicator that even they do not sufficiently believe in their collective initiatives.

As for the failure at the implementation stage, simple logic dictates that if the signing was imposed, then the implementation should also have been imposed. The guarantors and the regional powers abandoned their obligations to do the obvious.

The implementation process was bound to fail, and it did fail. Time has proven us right. The South Sudanese conflict has defeated the region and the world. As stated earlier, even the US Envoy, Ambassador Donald Booth publicly acknowledged the staggering failure of his government to resolve it.

For us, it was good thing that Salva Kiir did not hide his fascist intentions. He publicly declared that he would not implement an agreement he signed under duress. True to his words, Kiir scrapped ARCSS in full view of the world and rejuvenated his despotic regime through intimidation of all the parties. This included JMEC, whose technocrats with the best institutional memory of the agreement were declared persona non-grata within three weeks of the onset of the implementation phase.

Mr. Aly Verjee and Ato Ebdeta, who helped draft ARCSS, were the first to be expelled from Juba for knowing too much. In fact, it was their punishment for drafting an agreement that was not palatable to the regime. Subsequently, poor JMEC succumbed to the whims of Kiir, who eventually reduced its Chairman, President Festus Mogea, to a mouthpiece of the regime.

Subsequently, the international community resigned itself to lackluster diplomacy. The easiest way to bring peace to South Sudan became the isolation of bona fide signatories to ARCSS like Dr. Machar of the SPLM (IO), Mr. Pagan Amum of the SPLM (FDs) and Dr. Lam Akol of National Alliance. This paved the way for Kiir to hand pick any poodle he felt comfortable with to implement nothing but his reservation in the agreement.

The dire consequences of that diplomatic fiasco have been increasing famine, the spread and intensification of the war, the refugee crisis and more genocide in our helpless communities throughout the country. In moral and legal terms, the regional and the international powers cannot be exonerated from that human tragedy. It was their failure to bring tangible pressure to bear on the intransigent party.

So far, we have learned that propping up the government in Juba and polishing its legitimacy with a dose of political dialogue and a dash of power sharing will not end the conflict. The parties must politically engage in a serious dialogue on structural and principle issues to resolve the conflict. Political commitments must also match political rhetoric.

The country needs a fundamental reworking of the governance arrangements among the parties if a negotiated settlement is to lead to a sustainable peace. Mediation is most successful when practiced by a lead mediator, ideally representing a single institution and grounded with a clear mandate. The one chosen to lead should fully understand the specifics of the conflict and be capable of an honest assessment of the comparative inherent advantages and disadvantages within the dynamics of the conflict

Once determined, coordination among a wider set of mediators is then critical to developing a coherent process. This should include consistent political messaging, resource support, and a division of labor. That was what made the Khartoum process more effective than that in Addis Ababa during the Face-to-Face phase.

Two other important dynamics merit reiteration on any assessment of the IGAD peace process. Each of these complicated the job of the mediators. The first was a lack of consensus among the parties, the mediating institution, and the wider community of supporters as to the nature of the conflict itself and thus to the scope and depth of its solution.

In any case, my own take on IGAD mediation is that multi-state mediation has proven to be the most dangerous model to use for conflict resolution. The mediators in question use the very peace forum as a platform to promote their own interests instead of focusing on the conflict under discussion. That was the case during the last round of shuttle diplomacy between Kampala and Khartoum. The negotiations were turned into Sudan and Uganda arm-wrestling over their respective interests.

Sudan needed to accomplish two things urgently: To secure the flow of oil to fix its deteriorating economy and to use the agreement to bail itself out in Washington D.C. They also desperately wanted to get off the hook from sanctions and decades of diplomatic isolation.

Meanwhile, Uganda wanted to consolidate Kiir's power in Juba and avert looming sanctions on itself over the arms embargo against Juba.

Secondly, there was the political and moral dilemma faced by outside players when they realize a conflict is not "ripe" for settlement. This is when tradeoffs are made between 'ideal solutions' and the imperative to stop the violence.

The South Sudanese conflict is not ripe for solution as long the current despot in Juba continues to deal with it through fake political accommodation and coercion to maintain the status quo without addressing the grievances of the opposition. Salva Kiir and company keeps forgetting that if ministerial positions were enabled to address grievances, some people, including this author, would not have left government jobs to join the opposition. We are for a lasting solution that comes through addressing the root causes of the conflict through institutional reforms and a democratic transformation of the political process.

CHAPTER NINETEEN

Conclusions
and the Way Forward

Although the IGAD rag-tagged mediation has miserably failed to expeditiously resolve the on going crisis in South Sudan, it has given South Sudanese leaders a forum to dialogue and save their nascent nation from eminence death. Thematic to the core are: restoration of peace and stability through accountability, reparation and reconstruction as stipulated in the ARCISS. The ARCSS or R-ARCSS for that matter remains relevant as the parties can derive their legitimacy only from the terms of that Agreement. This explains why the government professes its continuing adherence to the agreement while routinely violating its terms. The ARCSS is the most encompassing panacea to fix South Sudan and give the people an opportunity to mend the rifts on the social fabric of their society, write their own constitution and choose their own leaders in a free and fair election at the end of the three year transitional period. According to the matrix of Revitalized Agreement on the Conflict Resolution in South Sudan(R_ARCSS), the agreement provides a fixed timetable to end the life span of Kiir's regime, concluding it with elections 60 days before the end of the Transitional Government of National Unity. In fact, those of us who negotiated that agreement conceptualized the whole deal as a negotiated leadership transition to create the South Sudanese state we aspire to have as a people. Call it a constructive regime change if you will.

It leaves no doubt in my mind that the sponsors (TRIOKA) or friends of IGAD meant well to help the people of South Sudan to attain lasting peace in their own country. Unfortunately, the supposedly lifesaving process has brought more death and destruction to the people of South Sudan. It has prolonged the suffering of our people as the guarantors of this process have abandoned their responsibility at the implementation stage leaving the victims of this destructive war to fend for themselves. That is serious disservice to the taxpayers in the sponsoring nations and the downtrodden people of South Sudan. The current lackluster diplomacy makes matters even worse for our people. This diplomacy of doing nothing by saying something is disastrous as it sends a wrong signal to the regime and its allies in the region that the international community can only talk the talk as another way to continue doing nothing. The decay of this lackluster diplomacy was read loud and clear in the recently issued joint statement by United States, United Kingdom, Norway known as TRIOKA declaring that they can not directly involve in the Khartoum Peace process but can join in depending on the progress made along the way. This means, they will continue to condemn none implementation of the ceasefire and humanitarian crisis without doing any thing tangible about it. We have been here before and have known by now that condemnation cannot deter the wrath of the fascist regime in Juba.

Although the region and the international community have the moral responsibility to hold the parties to account of what they signed, the responsibility squarely rests on the shoulder of the South Sudanese political leaders and their parties. The political leaders on both side of the dichotomy must come to their senses and understand that they do not have another country, but this one and together. Whatever the mediated dialogue may produce must be collectively owned by the South Sudanese themselves. Otherwise, no peace will be successfully imposed from outside South Sudan. If any thing, the peace process can be used as a Nyaproject mi thin (small project) in the word of Dr. Peter Adwok Nyaba by entrepreneurs in the field of conflict resolution.

My own reading and discernment as a practiced diplomat myself has been that the neighboring states have converted the South Sudanese peace process into a diplomatic forum to pursue vital interests of their own states. So depending on them to bring peace to South Sudan without us internalizing it is also another dangerous illusion. As mentioned in the prior chapters, the predicament of South Sudan is squarely that of the politicized militarism. This must be shunned through a politically negotiated settlement and serious confidence building through dialogue. South Sudan must be transformed into a talking nation to discard the prevailing habitual preoccupation with violent and barbaric militarism. It goes without stressing that there is nothing wrong with the military as a profession. We also recognize the heroic armed struggle under the SPLM/A and other armed historical movements since the heydays of Anyanya culminating in the independence of South Sudan. The abomination is the inherent lack of professionalism, discipline and patriotism on the part of our armed forces. Experiences elsewhere bear out the bitter truth that Political Militarism akin to that of the SPLM/A breeds nothing but perennial political violence. Hence, I submit that we must first and foremost demilitarize politics and engage in dialogue with cold minds aiming at creating a permanent cultural environment of free dialogue, not only among the political and military elites but also among the grass root communities of South Sudan. This must be done and the time is now. Otherwise, the very viability of South Sudan as a nation will be hanging in the balance for even longer time to come. It is that dialogue and civic education that will demilitarize the minds to demilitarize the towns and cure this chronic pathology of violent and tribal militarism. In sum, we must start to look inward for solution because the solution is within us and can be cultivated only through genuine peace talks, not war talks under duress from the outside world.

Bibliography

African Union (2014) *Final Report of the African Union Commission of Inquiry on South Sudan*, 15 October, p. 21. This report exposed the role of the President and the Government in the atrocities committed in Juba between December 15 and 18, 2013

Donald Booth, "*South Sudan's Peace Process: Reinvigorating the Transition*" Chatham House, London, UK, February 9, 2016.

The UN Security Council Resolution 2241 (October 9, 2015), UN Doc. S/RES/2241.

The members of the Panel of Experts established pursuant to Security Council resolution 2206 (2015), whose mandate was extended pursuant to Council resolution 2290 (2016) submitted its report in accordance with paragraph 12 (e) of resolution 2290 (2016), the Panel's 120-day report.

Peace and Security Council 515th Meeting at the Level of Heads of State and Government. Johannesburg, South Africa, PSC/AGH/2 (DXV),13 June, p. 3.

Zacharia Akol, "Inclusivity: A Challenge to the IGAD-Led South Sudanese Peace Process,"The Sudd Institute, December 7, 2014. www.suddinstitute.org/assets/Publications/572b7eb3a4aeb_InclusivityAChallengeToTheIGADLedSouth_Full.pdf.

Agreement on the Resolution of the Conflict in South Sudan (ARCSS, 2015).

TRIOKA and EU Condemnations against the systematic violation of ARCISS by Kiir's regime since October 2015.

South Sudan: The Crisis of Infancy by Peter Adwok Nyaba (2016).

The Root Causes of December 2013: The SPLM Factor by Mabior Garang De Mabior.

Addis Agreements. By Jon de Ngong.

SPLM Position IGAD PLUS Mediated Peace Process for Sustainable Peace in South Sudan (July 6th, 2015, Nairobi, Kenya).

Intra-SPLM Dialogue: The Arusha Communique (January 21, 2015 Arusha,

Tanzania).

The Tragedy of South Sudan - The Way Forward by Dr. Amir Idri.s

https://www.nycbar.org/images/stories/pdfs/.../s_sudan_dridris_ presentation.pdf

15. When Victims Become Killers Colonialism, Nativism, and the Genocide in Rwanda Mahmood Mamdani. Editions. Paperback. 2002. 39.95. 30.00. ISBN.

16. "South Sudan: The Road to Civil War" with Professor Mahmood ...

https://sites.tufts.edu/.../south-sudan-the-road-to-civil-war-with-professor-mahmood-m...

17. A Poisoned Well: Lessons in Mediation from South Sudan's Troubled Peace Process -

Zach Vertinr.

18. Southern Sudan: Too Many Agreements Dishonored by Honorable Abel Alier (Paul and Pub Consortium, September 29th, 1992).

19. Politics of Liberation by Peter A. Nyaba (2000).

20. The African-Arab Conflict in the Sudan, by Dunstan M. Wai (1978).

https://www.foreignaffairs.com/reviews/capsule-review/.../african-arab-conflict-sudan

21. Democide: Death by Government, By John Rummel, (NJ, 1994).

22. IGAD, "Communiqué of the 24th Extra-ordinary IGAD Summit on South Sudan," Addis Ababa, January 31, 2014.